THE PRISONER OF LOVE

The Earl looked at her searchingly and then he said:

"I want a wife to belong to me completely. To be mine exclusively for all time!"

He paused before he said very quietly:

"And I think, Sorilda, I have found her."

Then, as in some miraculous dream, he bent forward and gently sought her lips. It was a tender kiss, almost as a man might touch a flower.

"I . . . love you!" she wanted to cry.

Again the Earl looked at her searchingly.

"Peter said you were the Sleeping Beauty," he said and his voice was deep. "I can promise you, my darling, that I am the man who is going to awaken you."

As he spoke his lips found hers. But now he kissed her fiercely, passionately, with new urgency.

Suddenly, a little flame of fire awoke within her. It flickered and burned its way through her body, up from her breasts and into her throat.

Teach me," she whispered. "Teach me . . . how to love you."

Bantam books by Barbara Cartland
Ask your bookseller for the books you have missed

Barbara Cartland
The Prisoner of Love

THE PRISONER OF LOVE
A Bantam Book / June 1979

ISBN 0-553-12792-6

Published simultaneously in the United States and Canada

Bantam Books are published by Bantam Books, Inc. Its trademark, consisting of the words "Banam Books" and the por-
trayal of a bantam, is Registered in U.S. Patent and Trademark
Office and in other countries. Marca Registrada. Bantam
Books, Inc., 666 Fifth Avenue, New York, New York 10019.

PRINTED IN THE UNITED STATES OF AMERICA

Author's Note

The details of the opposition to the building of the Crystal Palace in 1851 and the details of the Great Exhibition are all correct.

Beyond all blessings was the vindication of Prince Albert. In transports of relief and delight, the Queen poured out the fullness of her heart to King Leopold of Belgium.

"It was the *happiest, proudest* day in my life, and I can think of nothing else. Albert's dearest name is immortalised with his *great* conception, *his* own, and my own dear country showed she was *worthy* of it."

The Prisoner of Love

Chapter One

1851

The Duke of Nuneaton rustled *The Morning Post* before he said in an irritated tone.

"I see Winsford has been given the Garter. God knows what he has done to deserve it!"

As he spoke he put the newspaper down on the silver holder which stood in front of his place at the breakfast-table and occupied himself with eating a plateful of sweetbreads in a manner which told the two women sitting on either side of him that he was extremely irritated.

"The Earl certainly has a leg which will show the Garter to advantage!" the Duchess said.

She spoke in a deliberately soothing tone, but her husband looked up from his plate to say sharply:

"You would stick up for the fellow! It was quite obvious at the State Ball last week what you thought about him."

The Duchess raised her eye-brows and replied in what her Step-niece thought of as her "little-girl voice":

"What can you mean, Edmund dear? I was sure you would wish me to be polite to a near neighbour."

The Duke growled something beneath his breath and went on eating his breakfast.

1

Sorilda, listening, knew that her Uncle was jealous and she thought it was not surprising.

It had been as much of a shock to her as it had been to everybody else at the Castle three months ago when the Duke, a week after his sixtieth birthday, announced his marriage to a young widow thirty-five years younger than himself.

At first Sorilda had thought that it might be rather fun to have someone nearer her own age in the house and that she and her Step-aunt would be friends.

She was swiftly disillusioned.

Iris had no use for women and certainly not for those who might in any way be rivals to her.

It never struck Sorilda that that was what she might seem to be to her aunt, and she was prepared to admire the new Duchess's beauty whole-heartedly, until she learnt all too quickly that it was what her Nurse had always described as "only skin-deep."

Six months after her Uncle's marriage, Sorilda faced the fact that the home she had found after her parents' death had been changed into, as far as she was concerned, a miserable and unhappy place where she found herself dreading each new day.

The Duke, besotted as only an elderly man can be with a young wife, could see nothing but the seductive charms of the woman he had married, and he had no idea that to other people in the Castle she was a dragon breathing fire and leaving tears and unhappiness forever in her wake.

It seemed extraordinary, Sorilda had often thought to herself, that while externally Iris looked like anyone's preconceived idea of an angel, inside she should personify the devil himself.

Sorilda was unusually intelligent for a young girl because she had spent so much time with her father, who had been an outstandingly brilliant man.

He had been Captain of the Oppidans at Eton, had taken a First at Oxford, and when he entered Parliament he had been spoken of as the most outstanding young politician of his generation.

The whole nation proclaimed it a tragedy when Lord Lionel Eaton and his wife were killed in a railway-accident in France when on their way to a Political Conference.

To Sorilda her life crashed unexpectedly about her ears.

Although her Uncle had tried to be kind and had taken her to live in his Castle in Northamptonshire, she had for a long time found it impossible to do anything but mourn the loss of the father and mother, whom she had loved.

Looking back, she thought that her home had always been a place of light and laughter, and she had known that more than anything else it was because there was an atmosphere of love there which she certainly did not find in the Castle.

Her Uncle had been a widower for ten years. His sons were grown up and married, the oldest, the Marquis, having already made his mark as a diplomat, being the Viceroy of India.

The Duke led an extremely busy life. Not only was he constantly in attendance on the Queen at Buckingham Palace, but he was also Lord Lieutenant of Northamptonshire and held an inordinate number of official posts in the County.

It had never struck Sorilda, let alone other people, that he was in fact a lonely man and, like many men before him, longed to grasp the pleasures of youth before he was too old to enjoy them.

He was therefore in exactly the right frame of mind for somebody like Mrs. Iris Handley, who was looking round for a fitting position to grace her beauty.

She had, of course, a large number of admirers, but the majority, being married men, were unable to offer her what she craved, another gold ring on her finger.

She had met the Duke at a large dinner-party when she had found herself, by one of those quirks of fate for which there is no explanation, sitting next to him.

The Duke's partner as planned, an elderly woman of great distinction, had been taken ill at the very last moment, and rather than reseating the whole table, the hostess had just put Iris Handley in her place.

It was not surprising that the Duke, who invariably found himself as he had once said, having to escort "the Mayor's wife" into dinner, found it an agreeable surprise to be seated next to one of the most beautiful women he had ever seen.

Men were usually bowled over at their first sight of Iris.

Her pale blue eyes, her fair hair, and her pink-and-white complexion were the average man's ideal of what a woman should look like, especially when the Queen had set the fashion in everything that was small, sweet, and feminine.

The Duke was not aware of it that evening, but when Iris's blue eyes looked into his, he was a lost man.

It was Sorilda who first sensed that her new Step-aunt's appearance belied her nature.

Iris and the Duke were married so quickly that there was no time for her to visit Nuneaton Castle before she became the Duchess.

The Duke had therefore brought her back to the traditional rejoicings—a feast for the tenants in the Tythe Barn, arches of welcome erected in the village and up the drive, and a display of fireworks as soon as it was dark.

When Iris had stepped out of the carriage earlier in the day, wearing the widest crinoline that Sorilda had ever seen, a taffeta pelisse which matched her eyes, and a bonnet trimmed with small ostrich-feathers of the same colour, she had gasped at her beauty.

Then she ran forward spontaneously to curtsey to her Uncle and put her arms round his neck as she said:

"Congratulations, Uncle Edmund! I do hope you will be very, very happy! We have all been so excited to meet your bride!"

"Then you must meet her, my dear," the Duke replied good-humouredly.

He turned to his wife and said:

"This is my niece, Sorilda, who lives with me. I am sure you will be good friends."

"*Lives* with you?"

There was a note in the question that made Sorilda stiffen.

Surely, she thought, her Uncle would have told his wife that she lived in the Castle?

"Yes, yes," the Duke replied. "Sorilda's parents died in the most tragic circumstances. I have not yet had time to tell you about it, my dearest."

Sorilda, having curtseyed, was waiting, and as she saw the expression in the Duchess's eyes, she felt as if there were a sudden cold wind blowing round her shoulders.

The Duke, in his joy at showing his new wife her future home, noticed nothing.

Taking her hand, he led her up the steps and into the Hall, where the vast array of servants was lined up to receive her.

She was very gracious, accepting the congratulations and the good wishes with a smile on her lovely face which Sorilda was later to think would deceive anybody except those who knew her well.

It was extraordinary how one woman could completely alter the atmosphere of a building as impressive and historic as the Castle within a few weeks of her arrival.

And yet Iris contrived to do just that.

It was not only what she said. It was the manner in which she grasped power with the avid greed of a fanatically ambitious woman.

Nothing and no-one should stand in her way. Everything would be exactly as she wished it to be.

The Castle had always been rather gloomy and everything in it moved slowly, as if time was of no particular importance.

Suddenly it was galvanized into new life, and

although some of the innovations were good, the way that they were introduced and the manner in which the new mistress extracted obedience were revolutionary.

Several of the older servants were pensioned off with barely enough time to realise what was happening, and this alone created a feeling of unease amongst the others.

Sorilda could sense it in the manner in which they moved about the house more quickly but nervously, and she had a feeling that their security had been snatched from them when they least expected it.

As far as Sorilda was concerned, Iris wasted no time in showing her very clearly that she had no wish to chaperone her husband's niece.

Sorilda was not in the least conceited, but she would have been very stupid if she had not realised that her own good looks were the cause of the new Duchess's instantaneous dislike of her.

Her mother had had Austrian blood in her and she had inherited the dark red hair that was peculiar to the great Viennese beauties. Her eyes were distinctly green and her skin, as might be expected, had the softness of a magnolia-petal.

In the three years since her father and mother's death, when she had come to live in the Castle, Sorilda had grown from a pretty fifteen-year-old child into a beauty who undoubtedly would have been acclaimed had she ever gone to London.

The Duke had not yet thought there was any necessity for her to embark on a social life as she seemed quite content at the Castle.

Vaguely at the back of his mind he told himself that sooner or later she must be presented to the Queen at Buckingham Palace and he must find one of his less obnoxious relations to chaperone her.

The Duke had always been bored by the innumerable Eatons who fawned on him when they had the chance of meeting him and who were constantly bombarding him with letters that he seldom bothered to read.

Unlike his father, he did not envisage himself as head of the family, a father-figure for anyone who needed his assistance.

Instead he preferred to choose a few friends with whom he enjoyed associating and to keep everybody else at arm's length.

This meant that the visitors entertained at the Castle were usually of his own age, and because he made no effort to introduce Sorilda to anyone else, she was seldom invited to parties in the County.

This was also because most people were frightened of her Uncle.

He was in fact a very awe-inspiring man. He had been extremely handsome when he was young and the years had in no way lessened his appreciation of his own consequence.

He certainly considered himself to be head-and-shoulders above the ordinary people he met, and he saw no reason to entertain anyone who did not interest or amuse him.

This further limited those who were invited to the Castle, and Sorilda would have had a very bleak and lonely existence if it had not been that she was extremely concerned with her own education.

By conspiring with the Duke's Comptroller, who had been fond of her father, she had managed to have not only a Governess whom she liked, but she also had Tutors who came from many parts of the County to give her instruction.

If the Duke deprecated the high cost of her education he did not say so, and because Sorilda chose the subjects that interested her most, her education was, to all intents and purposes, that of a man rather than a young woman.

A year before, when she became seventeen, her Governess said that she thought it was time for her to leave, since otherwise she would be too old to find

another post. Consequently, Sorilda found herself very
much on her own, but she still kept up her music-
lessons, the Tutor who taught her modern languages,
and another with whom she studied the Classics.

She had thought, however, that she should make
her Uncle realise that she was grown up and could no
longer be kept in the School-Room.

Then Iris had arrived, and it had not taken long
for Sorilda to realise that she was to be kept no longer
in the School-Room but very much in the background.'

Like many beautiful women, Iris was quite unnecessarily jealous of any competition.

She had to hold the centre of the stage always, at
every conceivable moment of the day and night.

She viewed as a possible rival any woman who
was not positively old and hideous, and she was unpleasantly shocked by Sorilda's appearance as soon
as she reached the Castle.

Now as the Duke replied to his wife's remark,
Sorilda, in an effort to placate him, said:

"I think the reason why the Earl of Winsford
has been given the Garter is because he has supported Prince Albert from the very beginning in his
plans for the Crystal Palace."

"How can you possibly be aware of that?" the
Duchess asked.

Before Sorilda could reply, the Duke interposed:

"She is right, and a damned silly idea it is from
start to finish! Only a lunatic would think of designing
a Palace made of glass, and to desecrate Hyde Park
is the greatest fraud and the greatest imposition ever
thrust upon the people of this country!"

The Duke spoke angrily, but Sorilda remembered
that almost the same expressions had been used in the
House of Commons by one of the Members of Parliament.

Despite the opposition not only from distinguished personages like the Duke but also from the
newspapers, the building of the Crystal Palace had
gone ahead.

"You mark my words," the Duke was saying, his voice rising, "the whole thing will be a ghastly failure, and it will not surprise me if the building collapses at the very moment when Her Majesty is opening it!"

He gave a snort as he added:

"What can one expect from a gardener's boy who is allowed to call himself an architect?"

This referred, Sorilda knew, to Joseph Paxton, who was one of the most remarkable men of the century.

He had indeed started life as a gardener's boy, but he had become the protégé of the Duke of Devonshire and without architectural qualifications had become celebrated as the designer of the great Conservatory at Chatsworth, the Duke's seat in Derbyshire.

The newspapers had related scornfully that Paxton had produced for Prince Albert's inspection a rough sketch for the Palace of Glass, which was basically a greenhouse on an undreamt-of scale.

The Duke's prophesy of disaster was by no means the only one.

Sorilda read the newspapers very methodically and found innumerable articles, letters, and reports declaring that the building would collapse and the footsteps of the walking multitudes would start up vibrations that must shake it down.

A Member of Parliament, Colonel Charles Sibthorp, an arch-Tory, declared that the dearest wish of his heart was that "the confounded building called Crystal Palace would be dashed to pieces."

Other people were certain that a hailstorm would crack it, thunder would shatter it, and rain would swamp it. But the building of Crystal Palace continued, and Sorilda had read that now that it was approaching completion, even the most adverse critics had begun to feel that something very extraordinary was about to take place.

The Queen was to open the Crystal Palace on May 1, which was only two weeks ahead.

From the very beginning the Duke had been one

of those violently against Prince Albert's "dream-child," although Sorilda was quite certain that he did not say so when he was at Buckingham Palace.

At this moment she was sure that it was not the Palace that was really annoying him, but the fact that he was jealous of the Earl of Winsford.

Because she was sensitive to what other people were feeling and was aware that her Step-aunt did not always disguise her emotions, she was sure that the Earl meant more to Iris than simply that his lands marched with those of the Castle.

When the Earl's name was mentioned, which was fairly frequently, there was a look in those pale blue eyes which Sorilda felt was different from the usual calculating glance with which she surveyed the world.

If the young Duchess was enamoured of the Earl of Winsford it would not be surprising.

Ever since she had come to live in the Castle, Sorilda had heard him talked about not only by her Uncle and his guests, but also by the servants, the farmers on the estate, the huntsmen, the woodsmen, and everybody else in the neighbourhood.

When she had seen the Earl for the first time at a Meet of Hounds which took place annually at the Castle, Sorilda had understood why so much gossip surrounded him.

Not only was he extremely handsome, which would account for the women's interest in him, but he rode better than any other man she had ever seen.

Living at the Castle, she had learnt that his horses were as outstanding as their master. He had won the Gold Cup at Ascot last year and was expected to win it again this year.

The Duke had been tolerant if not effusive about the Earl before he married, then overnight it seemed that the neighbour with whom he had always lived in peace became an enemy.

"I will tell you one thing," he was saying now, still in the hectoring tone he used when he was annoyed, "if we get through the opening ceremony of this ridiculous building without losing our lives or being cut to pieces by falling glass, I shall be exceedingly surprised!"

The Duchess laughed.

"I am not frightened, Edmund, and there is no reason for you to work yourself up about it being dangerous."

"It is not only dangerous, it is sheer lunacy!" the Duke retorted. "When I was in London two days ago, I was told the latest idiocy that is taking place in that monstrosity."

"What is that?" Sorilda asked eagerly.

She longed to see the Crystal Palace for herself, but when she had suggested that she might go to London for that sole purpose, her Step-aunt had made it very clear that she was to remain in the country and had categorically forbidden her to stay at Nuneaton House in Park Lane.

It was most unfair, Sorilda thought, when it seemed that everybody else in the whole of Northampton would be journeying to London for the Exhibition.

But it did not really surprise her, as she knew that her Step-aunt's feelings towards her were growing more vitriolic week by week, month by month.

"Do tell me what is happening, Uncle Edmund," she asked.

She was so curious that she ignored the frown on the smooth white forehead between the two exquisitely pale blue eyes because the Duchess felt that she was pushing herself forward.

As if he was rather glad to have the opportunity of further disparaging the Exhibition, the Duke said:

"It has been found that the three large elm-trees in the transept harbour so many sparrows that all the rich goods on display could be spoilt by them."

"Why on earth did they not think of that before they left the trees unfelled in the Palace?" Sorilda asked.

"You may well ask the question," the Duke re-

plied. "The whole conception is a disgrace from start
to finish, and when you think that an average of two
thousand workman have been working on this disastrous project, it makes me despair of our country's
sanity!"

"What have they done about the sparrows, Uncle
Edmund?" Sorilda enquired, wanting to keep the Duke
to the point.

"The Queen suggested that Lord John Russell
should be sent for," the Duke answered, "and Lord
John advised that soldiers from the Regiments of
Foot-Guards should be sent into the building to shoot
the sparrows."

"Surely that would break the glass?"

"That is what the Prince pointed out," the Duke
replied, annoyed that she had anticipated what he was
about to say.

"Then what did they do?"

"Somebody, I do not know who," the Duke answered, "suggested sending for the Duke of Wellington."

"And what did he suggest?"

"I believe he remarked that he was not a bird-
catcher, but on the Queen's command he presented
himself at Buckingham Palace."

With difficulty Sorilda prevented herself from in-
terrupting, as she knew by her Uncle's tone of voice
that he was coming to the point of the story.

The Duke paused a little, then after a glance at
his wife, to see if she was listening, he said:

"Wellington, I understand, uttered four words:
'Try sparrow-hawks, Ma'am.' "

Sorilda clapped her hands.

"Oh, that was clever, very clever of him!"

"And what happened?" the Duchess asked, because she felt that it was expected of her.

She was obviously not particularly interested because she never was unless the conversation involved
herself.

The Duke gave a short laugh.

"It was reported that the sparrows flew out of the Crystal Palace in a body and were never seen again!"

Sorilda laughed, and as her Uncle laughed too, she thought that he was in a better humour now that he had been able to tell her a story, which was something he always enjoyed.

For a moment he had forgotten the Earl of Winsford.

The Duchess rose to her feet.

"I am sure you have something better to do, Sorilda, than sit here at the breakfast-table," she said disagreeably. "Actually I have various tasks waiting for you in my *Boudoir*. Come with me and I will give them to you."

Sorilda had not quite finished her coffee, but she knew better than to delay, and she obediently followed the Duchess from the room, noticing, as she did so, how perfectly her crinoline swung from her small waist.

She was feeling a violent resentment because the Duchess had refused to allow the whalebone frame that supported Sorilda's gown to be wider than two feet from side-to-side.

It was extremely unfortunate that Iris had come into her Step-niece's life at a moment when Sorilda was in need of a number of new clothes, having grown out of her old ones.

She had in fact been planning a visit to London to buy what was necessary in the way of gowns and cloaks and with them new bonnets made fashionable by the Queen.

Then had come the Duke's surprise wedding, and the clothes had therefore gone unbought.

After the new Duchess's reign had begun, Sorilda had found it impossible to buy anything without first receiving her Step-aunt's approval.

"I have always chosen my own clothes," she protested.

"You must allow me to know what is best for you," Iris had replied firmly.

Sorilda had soon found that what Iris considered "best" for her was in every way to her disadvantage.

She soon became aware that the Duchess intended to do everything in her power to detract from her appearance.

She flatly refused to allow Sorilda's gowns to be made in anything but an unpleasant shade of fawn, which made her skin look sallow, or a drab grey which made her feel like a ghost.

It was no use appealing to her Uncle, for Sorilda knew that he was completely under his new wife's thumb and would agree to anything she suggested so long as she smiled at him and coaxed him in a manner which he found utterly irresistible.

It was not only by choosing her clothes that the Duchess tried to alter Sorilda's appearance.

She was astonished when one evening before she went down to dinner her Step-aunt's lady's-maid, a gaunt and unpleasant woman who Sorilda knew repeated to her mistress everything that happened belowstairs, came into her bedroom.

"Good-evening, Harriet!" Sorilda exclaimed, and waited to hear the reason for her appearance.

"Her Grace has asked me to do your hair in a new style, Miss."

"I am quite happy with the way it is now," Sorilda replied.

Harriet had not even bothered to answer her, and Sorilda, knowing that it was not a request but an order, sat down at her dressing-table.

Harriet produced a china pot which Sorilda looked at questioningly.

"Her Grace thinks your hair looks dry, Miss," Harriet explained.

Opening the pot, she started to smear Sorilda's hair with what appeared to be a dark pomade.

It was soon quite obvious that the result took away the colour of her hair and left it dank and limp.

It was then arranged by Harriet in a tight bun at

the back of her head with small and unbecoming plaits falling beside her cheeks to be looped up round her ears.

Sorilda said nothing, but she knew exactly what her Step-aunt was about, and was not at all certain what she could do about it.

It was only as she considered the whole situation that she began to realise how completely she was being excluded from meeting anyone or going anywhere, and she could see her whole life being spent in the Castle with no possible means of escape.

When they entertained, Iris made excuses for Sorilda not to come down to dinner.

"We are a man short and I cannot find anyone to make up the right numbers," she would say in front of the Duke, "so I know, dear child, you will understand and have dinner alone just this once."

The same thing would happen at luncheon-parties, and though Sorilda longed to protest and say it was not once but continually, she knew that whatever she said, her Step-aunt would find an answer and the Duke would support her.

She began to feel as if a trap was closing in on her and that she was being incarcerated in a prison in which she had a life-sentence.

Sometimes when the Duchess had been particularly unpleasant she would go to the window of her room and look out over the green Park, with its great ancient oak-trees extending to the far sky-line, and feel that she was behind bars.

This, she told herself, was how Royal prisoners felt when they were taken to some isolated Castle and knew there was no escape except by death.

"How can I bear it? How can I stay here forever when I am treated like this?" she asked herself.

But however hard she tried, she could find no loop-hole or pass-word to carry her through the invisible barriers which stood between her and freedom.

It was all the Duchess's doing, and yet Sorilda blamed herself that she had been foolish not to have talked to her Uncle about her future before he was married.

Never in her wildest dreams had she imagined, when he seemed to her so old and staid in his ways, that he would suddenly embark upon a new life with a young wife.

It was very obvious to Sorilda why Iris had married him, and because she was perceptive, or perhaps because she was a woman, she could see the efforts that Iris made to keep the Duke's attention and hold him a willing slave to her beauty.

Sometimes the mask that Iris wore slipped and Sorilda would know that she was bored and impatient with her elderly husband and that even the position of Duchess could not compensate her for the loss of the admirers who had circled round her in the past.

Sorilda was not quite certain when she first began to suspect that her Step-aunt was particularly interested in the Earl of Winsford.

Perhaps it was because when people spoke of him she noticed an unusual flicker of interest in those pale blue eyes and a sudden warmth in a voice that, when speaking to women, was usually coldly indifferent if not acidly unpleasant.

Whatever it was, Sorilda found herself looking for signs that Iris became more human when the Earl's name was mentioned.

Now as she followed the Duchess down the passage, Sorilda said:

"Are you going to write to the Earl and congratulate him on being made a Member of the Order of the Garter?"

She was behind her Step-aunt, and yet without seeing her face she felt that she was receptive to the idea.

There was a little pause before the Duchess replied:

"I am sure that would be the correct thing to do. I wonder if he is at home or in London."

"He is here at Winsford House."

"How do you know?"

The question was sharp.

"The grooms were talking about him yesterday, saying that he had brought down a new team of horses which he had purchased at Tattersall's."

As she spoke, Sorilda knew that the Duchess was in fact aware of the Earl's whereabouts.

She could not explain how she knew, it was just as if she was reading her Step-aunt's thoughts.

"Then we must certainly ask him to dinner," the Duchess exclaimed. "A small party would be delightful! But I only hope your Uncle will not rant on about the Crystal Palace."

They walked up the stairs and the Duchess led the way into her *Boudoir,* which adjoined the State-Room in which she slept.

The *Boudoir* was fragrant with flowers that came from the hot-houses in the walled-in garden, and there was also the aroma of an exotic French perfume, a fragrance which Iris left on the air wherever she went.

"Now let me see . . ." the Duchess was saying as she went to her *secrétaire,* which stood by one of the windows, "I doubt if His Lordship will stay long in the country, so I had better send my invitation by a groom. I will write it now, and you can carry it to the stables and tell Huxley to have it taken to Winsford House immediately."

Sorilda waited, knowing that the reason she was being given the letter was to prevent her Uncle from becoming aware of the dinner-party until it was too late for it to be cancelled.

As the Duchess wrote, Sorilda looked round the *Boudoir* and saw that Iris had accumulated in the room many of the best and most valuable pieces in the Castle.

There were the miniatures of the Nuneaton family which went back to Tudor times, the diamond-studded snuff-boxes that had been given to the previous Duke by the Prince Regent, and the onyx clock with jewelled hands and matching candlesticks.

There were innumerable other small objets d'art which had graced the Drawing-Rooms and other parts of the Castle before being moved here.

It was a fitting background for her beauty, Sorilda told herself honestly, yet she wondered, as she had done so often before, why anyone who had been blessed with such an exquisite face and a perfectly proportioned body should not have a heart and soul to match.

She was not the only person in the Castle who suffered from Iris's scheming for power and was punished for being attractive.

Maids who had no other fault but that they were comely had been dismissed without a reference, and Sorilda knew that the same would have been her own fate if it had been possible for her to be got rid of in the same manner.

The Duchess finished her letter, placed it in an envelope, and sealed it.

"Now hurry to the stables, Sorilda," she said sharply, "and when you have given Huxley the note, do not waste time with the horses but come straight back."

Sorilda did not reply. She took the note and walked across the room.

As she reached the door she looked back and saw an expression in the Duchess's eyes that made her shiver.

"Why should she hate me so?" she asked herself as she went down the stairs.

She could see her reflection in one of the long gilt-framed mirrors and thought that it was pitiable compared to the elegantly gowned, exquisitely beautiful Duchess.

Her greased-down hair and her drab fawn gown, which she wore over a sad imitation of a crinoline, made her look like a charity-child, or some poor shop-keeper's assistant.

The only thing Iris could not alter was Sorilda's eyes. Very large, so that they seemed to dominate her heart-shaped face, they gleamed green in the pale spring sunshine coming through the long windows of the Hall.

But in their depths Sorilda knew there was a darkness and despair because she was afraid.

"One day," she told her reflection as she passed the mirror, "I shall sink into such insignificance that I shall just cease to exist."

The thought was like a pain inside her, and although she tried not to think about it, it persisted.

When she reached the stables she gave the note to Huxley, the Head Groom.

"Her Grace asks that you take this immediately to Winsford House," Sorilda said.

"Th' horses won't be keen, Miss Sorilda; they doesn't like th' competition they finds there," the groom said jokingly.

This, Sorilda knew, was a somewhat familiar way of speaking. At the same time, the servants at the Castle still treated her as if she were the child she had been when she first arrived and they had tried to comfort her in her sad loss.

"I wish I could see the Earl's new horses," she said.

"Next time ye goes riding, Miss," Huxley answered, "take a look over the boundary at th' Burnt Oak."

"You mean he rides on the Long Gallop?"

"Mos' days when His Lordship's in th' country."

"Then if I get a chance I shall certainly look at him," Sorilda said with a smile. "He is a fine rider."

"Best Oi've ever seen!" Huxley agreed. "We're all a-backing him to win the Gold Cup, not that th' odds'll be worth 'aving."

"Be careful there is not an 'outsider' to slip past the post at the last moment," Sorilda teased.

She knew that Huxley was an inveterate gambler. In fact she had often discussed with him his different bets and was delighted when he had backed a winner.

"Now don' ye go a-frightenin' me, Miss Sorilda!"

Huxley protested. "It's a pity ye won't be attendin' Royal Ascot this year, as we'd expected."

Sorilda remembered that they had talked about it the previous year and she had told Huxley that she was sure, as she would be eighteen, that her Uncle would let her attend Ascot Races.

It was something she had always longed to do, but now, with the advent of the new Duchess, she knew that she was as likely to be in the Royal Enclosure at Ascot as she was to be at the North Pole.

As if he saw by the expression on her face that he had depressed her, Huxley said:

"Oi want ye to try out Kingfisher now that his fetlock's healed. He needs gentle handling. Oi daren't trust th' lads on him until he's back to his former self."

It was Huxley's way of being tactful, Sorilda knew, for she had always ridden Kingfisher before he had twisted a fetlock on one of the jumps.

"I will be ready at six o'clock tomorrow morning," she said.

"Oi'll be waitin' for ye, Miss Sorilda," Huxley replied. "It'll do ye good to have a bit o' exercise."

He was well aware why she had not been able to ride for several days.

The Duchess had forbidden her to ride when she might be running errands or doing some unpleasant task that was assigned to her more as a punishment than for any other reason.

At six o'clock in the morning she could slip out and reach the stables without anyone being aware of it.

Her only fear was that Harriet might see her and would undoubtedly make trouble by reporting it to her mistress.

Sorilda remembered now that she had been told not to linger at the stables.

"Six o'clock, Huxley," she said with a smile, "and thank you very much."

She was thanking him for far more than his promise to have Kingfisher ready for her, and as she walked away without looking back, the old groom was watching her, a worried expression in his eyes.

* * *

Sorilda went back to the Castle and as she reached the Hall she heard her Step-aunt calling to her from the top of the stairs:

"Come here!"

The Duchess's command was peremptory and Sorilda ran up the stairs quickly.

Taking her by the arm in a grip that hurt, the Duchess said:

"Did you tell Huxley to wait for an answer?"

"N-no," Sorilda replied, "you did not tell me to."

"Of course I meant him to do so, you little fool!" the Duchess said. "Run quickly and tell him to bring back an answer, and tell the footman to bring it to you, not to me. Do you understand?"

Just for a moment Sorilda's eyes widened, then without replying she went down the stairs quickly and back to the stables.

Now she knew that her suspicions about the Duchess's interest in the Earl were well founded, and she was certain that they had known each other before Iris had married the Duke.

In the stables she saw that one of the horses was already saddled and bridled, and a groom wearing her Uncle's livery was waiting to set off for Winsford House.

Huxley, with the note in his hand, was giving the lad instructions, and he turned his head in surprise as Sorilda reappeared.

"I forgot to say," she said to him in a low voice, "that the groom should wait for a reply and bring the note to me."

She felt embarrassed as she spoke, knowing that Huxley would be aware, from what they had already said, that she did not know the Earl, and it was quite obvious for whom the reply was really intended.

Huxley had been in private service all his life and well understood that however strange the behaviour of the Quality was, it was not for a servant to question it. So he simply replied:

"Very good, Miss. Oi expects Him'll be back within the hour, unless he has to wait o're-long."

"To save trouble," Sorilda replied, "I will come back to the stables in about an hour's time."

"Ye do that, Miss," Huxley answered, knowing that it would be a good excuse for her to be with the horses.

He gave the groom his instructions and Jim led the horse out of the cobbled yard and mounted.

"An' hurry back!" Huxley ordered. "Oi knows exac'ly how long it takes t' reach Winsford House!"

The groom grinned back at him, touched his cap to Sorilda, then rode through the arched entrance of the stables and started to trot down the drive.

"While I am here," Sorilda suggested, "let me have a look at Kingfisher."

Huxley took her eagerly into the horse's stable and Sorilda inspected the bandaged fetlock and talked to the horse in a way which made him nuzzle his nose against her.

"Six o'clock tomorrow morning," she said to Kingfisher, and felt that somehow he understood.

*   *   *

It was actually a little earlier when Sorilda, riding Kingfisher, left the stables by the other entrance, just in case anyone was looking out the windows of the Castle and should see her go.

Huxley had Kingfisher ready for her even though she was early, having awakened with a feeling of excitement because she could go riding.

She had slipped on her riding-habit, but because she knew that nobody would see her at that hour, she had not put on her hat.

Instead, she had arranged her hair as she used to do, with ringlets on either side of her face. But she knew that the pomade that Harriet had applied made them less curly and certainly less attractive than they had looked in the past.

However, there would be no-one to see her except Huxley and Kingfisher, and she knew that they both loved her not for her looks but because of the feelings she had for them, which came from her heart.

She knew it was important to ride Kingfisher very gently, not allowing him to break into a gallop but keeping him to a light trot.

So early in the morning there was a mist under the trees and hovering over the lowest parts of the Park.

The daffodils were in bloom and the first green buds were beginning to show on the trees.

It had been a harsh winter and everything was rather later than usual, and in consequence, Sorilda thought, all the more welcome.

She loved the spring. It always seemed to her to renew a feeling of hope and faith in the world beyond this one.

It also told those who were willing to hear that nothing was lost, nothing died that would not be re-born.

'Perhaps it will be a spring for me too,' she thought to herself.

She remembered how last year, even though she was often lonely without her father and mother, she had felt, because she was growing up, that there were new vistas, new horizons ahead of her.

It had been an optimism that was completely un-justified, and instead of going forward she now felt that she was going backwards.

Last week a blow that she had half-expected had fallen when her Step-aunt had told her that it was a sheer waste of money for her to continue with her Teachers and Tutors.

"You are too old for any more education," she

said. "Anyway, what is the point of all that learning?"

"There is so much more I want to know," Sorilda answered. "Please let me go on, at least with my
music."

"Who do you think will want to listen to you?"
Iris replied sharply. "Besides, your Uncle cannot af-
ford it."

This was untrue, but Sorilda knew that Iris required her Uncle to spend every penny on her and her
alone.

Never had she imagined that any woman in such
a short space of time could have collected such a large
amount of clothes and jewellery.

Some of the jewellery was in fact the Nuneaton
heirlooms, but there were a number of new pieces
which she had persuaded the Duke to give her, because
for the moment he could refuse her nothing.

It seemed extraordinary, Sorilda thought, that
with a trousseau and jewels that must have cost a
small fortune, she could deliberately constrict and re-
strain her husband's niece not only from having attractive gowns but also from enriching her mind.

"Please . . . please," she begged, "let me continue
with my music, at least until the end of the summer."

"No!" The Duchess's lips were set in a hard
line. Then her eyes narrowed.

"You must learn to do as you are told," she said,
"and be grateful that you have a roof over your head.
I should have thought there were plenty of relations who would be willing to have you live with
them."

"You must talk to Uncle Edmund about that,"
Sorilda answered.

She knew as she spoke that the Duke, who disliked his relations, would pay no attention to Iris's
suggestion that she should be sent away.

After she had spoken, she thought it would be
better for her to go even to an elderly cousin who did
not want her.

Nothing could be worse than staying here and being subjected day after day to the petty spitefulness of her new Step-aunt.

Then she told herself that not even that way was there an escape open.

The Duke, loathing his relations, would certainly not wish to communicate with them about her, and it would hurt his pride to have to tell them that she could not continue to live with him at the Castle.

Riding was the only time that she had a chance to escape, the only time that she could be alone and not expect a peremptory summons to do something unnecessary for her Step-aunt.

She rode away from the house and as she did so, she remembered how Huxley had said that if she wished to see the Earl, she would find him at the Long Gallop near the Burnt Oak.

This landmark was a tree that had been struck many years ago by lightning, but the burnt trunk still remained standing, and so many directions on the estate started by: "Turn right"—"Turn left"—or, "Go north" from the Burnt Oak.

Half-an-hour's riding brought her to the boundary-fence which divided the estates of the Duke and the Earl.

The Duke's land extended a long distance to the east and south. Only in the west was he constrained by the estate which had belonged to the Winsford family for generations.

Just over the boundary there was a long, flat piece of ground that was always known as the "Long Gallop."

The previous Earl had used it for training his race-horses but Sorilda had heard that his son was now constructing a race-course on another part of his estate.

She knew from the stable-talk that it was not yet finished and she was therefore not surprised, as she drew Kingfisher in under the shade of some trees, to see someone riding at a tremendous speed on the Long Gallop.

He was some distance from her and she watched his approach with interest, thinking that it must be a year since she had last seen the Earl and thought he was not only the most handsome man she had ever seen but certainly the best rider.

He flashed past her and she had an impression of superb horse-flesh and a rider who seemed to be part of his horse.

"I wonder if that is one of his new purchases," Sorilda asked herself.

Then the Earl drew his mount to a standstill and turned round to pass by her again.

Now he was moving much more slowly and she had a chance to see the horse clearly and appraise it as she wished to do.

It was a magnificent chestnut with a long mane and tail, and every muscle under its shining coat rippled, proclaiming it to be a thoroughbred in first-class condition.

Although she did not realise it, the chestnut was just a little lighter in colour than her own hair.

Now that she had inspected the horse, Sorilda, hidden by the overhanging branches of the trees, looked at the rider.

Perhaps it was because she was older now, or because she had heard a certain amount about him in the last year, but she certainly saw him now in a new light.

"He is attractive," she told herself, "so attractive that he could undoubtedly be dangerous to any woman who lost her heart to him!"

Chapter Two

The previous day, riding across country Jim had reached the Park of Winsford House in well under the time Huxley had expected.

As he saw the huge house which had been re-modelled at the beginning of the century, he thought it was not only one of the most impressive buildings he had ever seen, but he also knew that the stables in every way exceeded those of the Castle.

He rode down the drive, crossed the bridge over the lake, and turned right towards the side of the house where the kitchens and servants' quarters were situated.

Knowing Winsford House well, Jim knew where he could tie up his horse, and having done so, he walked to the kitchen-door.

He knocked and walked in, looking for someone to whom he could give the note which he had brought with him. Then he saw a familiar figure coming out of the room which he knew was the Servants' Hall, and he gave a shout.

"Betsy!"

An attractive face was turned to his and there was no doubt from her cry that she was pleased to see him.

"Hello, Jim! I weren't expecting you t'day!"

"Oi wasn't expectin' to come 'ere meself," Jim answered. "How are ye getting on?"

"All right," Betsy answered. "But it's not the same as being at th' Castle, an' a-knowing you're in th' stables."

"Oi miss ye too," Jim said in a low voice. "Oi was terrified when her sent ye away that ye'd 'ave t' go further afield than this."

" 'Twere kind of Cook to take I on," Betsy said. "She said as how she'd give I a chance, seein' as she knew me Dad when he were a boy."

Jim's lips tightened in a hard line.

He had been appalled, as had been every other servant in the Castle, when Betsy, whose family had served the Castle for three generations, had been thrown out by the new Duchess, for no reason that anyone could ascertain, and without a reference.

As if she was upset by the expression on his face, Betsy said:

" 'Tis all right, Jim. I'm happy enough here, so long as I can see you sometimes."

"Ye'll see me all right," Jim promised, "if Oi has anything t' do wi' it!"

"Mind you, being in th' kitchen ain't the same as being in th' house, but I were lucky t' be employed at all with nought t' recommend I."

Betsy could not help the resentment in her voice.

Every servant knew that it was extremely important from the very moment they went into service to have a good reference.

The Duchess's way of dismissing those she did not like, without explanation and without the all-important reference which would ensure them employment elsewhere, was talked about not only in the Castle but over the whole estate.

"Mr. Huxley says ye were sent away 'cause you're too pretty, an' Her Grace would get rid o' Miss Sorilda, given half a chance!"

"I knows that," Betsy exclaimed. "I've heard the way she speaks t' her. Made me fair sick, listening to it, seeing as how Miss Sorilda's never been anythin' but kind to everyone."

"That's roight," Jim agreed. "Me Mum says Her Ladyship were just th' same."

Betsy gave a deep sigh.

"It just goes t' show, don't it? A man should be careful who he marries."

"Oi intend t' be careful," Jim said. "That's why Oi'm a-going t' marry ye!"

"Oh, Jim, it'll be years afore we can save enough for that. Besides, if you're still working at th' Castle, I don't suppose Her Ladyship'd let you marry me."

"Then Oi'll find somewhere else t' work," Jim replied. "Nobody's goin' t' stop Oi marryin' ye, Oi can promise ye that!"

He put his arms round Betsy as he spoke, but when he would have kissed her, she looked over her shoulder in a frightened fashion.

"Not here!" she said. "Please, Jim, not here!"

"Where, then? An' when?"

"Tomorrow night. I'll slip out after supper an' meet you at th' end of th' drive."

"Oi'll be there, an' don' be late like ye were last time."

She smiled at him and then, as if she heard footsteps coming down the passage, began to move away.

"Here! Half a mo—!" Jim cried. "Ye 'aven't asked what Oi came for."

He put his hand in his pocket and brought out the note.

"For 'His Nibs,' from Her Grace!" he announced. "An' Oi'm t' wait for an answer."

Betsy took the note.

"I'll take it to th' Pantry," she said. "You'd better wait in th' Servants' Hall."

"Come back quick as ye can," Jim said in a low voice.

As Betsy hurried away down the passage, he strolled without haste into the large Servants' Hall with its long table down the centre of it.

Betsy walked along the passage towards the Pantry.

She had gone a little way before she glanced down at the letter she held in her hand and thought that the Duchess was like all the other women who were always running after His Lordship because he was so good-looking.

'Like flies round a honey-pot, they be!' Betsy thought scornfully.

At the same time, she admitted that His Lordship was certainly handsome enough to attract any woman, whoever she was.

Because she admired her new employer she thought it was a pity from his point of view that he should become involved with the Duchess of Nuneaton.

Betsy was a good-natured, even-tempered girl, but the unjust way in which she had been treated had struck her a blow from which she had not yet recovered.

Not only had she lost her job, but she felt that she had let down her parents, who had always been so proud of their service at the Castle, and also humiliated herself in front of all her friends on the estate and in the village.

She had gone to work for the Duke with so much pride, flaunting herself in front of the other girls with whom she had played as a child, because it had been a rule for several generations that the children whose fathers or mothers were already in service at the Castle should have preference over everybody else.

Then, when Mrs. Bellows, the Housekeeper, was pleased with her and she thought she was getting really proficient in her duties as sixth under-housemaid, she found herself sent away and for no reason except that the Duchess wished her to leave.

'I hates her!' Betsy thought now, looking down at the Duchess's rather flamboyant hand-writing.

She turned the envelope over, and as she did so,

she saw that the seal with which the Duchess had fastened the envelope was cracked.

It must have been the way Jim had thrust it into his pocket, she thought, and hoped he would not get into any trouble because the flap of the envelope was now open.

Even as Betsy looked at it and worried about Jim, a sudden idea came to her.

For a moment she thought it was too outrageous even to be considered. Then impulsively, driven by a curiosity and some other feeling beyond her control, she left the passage and opened the door that led into the Flower-Room.

There were shelves holding some of the innumerable cases that were used for the flowers that the gardeners brought in from the hot-houses all the year round.

It was empty now, and Betsy, shutting the door behind her, stood for a moment staring at the envelope in her hand.

Holding her breath because she knew that she was doing something so shocking that she was ashamed even to think of it, she drew from the envelope the thick sheet of crested writing-paper on which the Duchess had written her note.

Betsy had been to School, for the Duke provided one for the children of his employees in the village nearest the Castle and paid a School-Mistress to teach them.

She could therefore read, though slowly, and it took her a little time to decipher the Duchess's message, even though her hand-writing was large and clear.

Somewhat laboriously she read:

He will be away tomorrow night. Come at nine o'clock to the door of the West Tower, which I will leave open for you. It will be hard to wait until then, but I shall be longing to see you, to hear your voice, and to be in your arms.

There was no signature, but as Betsy finished reading the note she let out her breath in an audible gasp.

"Really!" she said to herself. "If His Grace knew what was a-going on he'd have a bit o' a surprise, seeing as how he fair dotes on that new wife o' his!"

She slipped the letter back into the envelope, wet her finger and pressed hard on the seal, and hoped that no-one would notice that it was cracked.

Then she went farther along the passage towards the Pantry.

It was only as she was hurrying back towards the Servants' Hall, where Jim was waiting, that an idea came to her which was so fantastic that she told herself she must be demented even to think of such a thing.

She opened the door of the Servants' Hall and for a moment she thought that Jim had gone without waiting for the reply which she had told the Butler to bring him.

Then he pounced on her from behind the door and, taking her in his arms, kissed her until she had to struggle to free herself.

"You behave yourself, Jim Tavel," she cried in a voice that tried vainly to be fierce and succeeded only in being rather breathless. "Get me th' sack, that's what you'll do. S'posing someone came in an' found us?"

"No-one did, an' Oi can't wait till Friday," Jim said.

He spoke with so much feeling in his voice that Betsy gave him a little smile, knowing how much he loved her and had done so ever since they had first grown up together.

As he reached out towards her again, she said:

"I hears His Grace be a-goin' away tomorrow."

"First Oi've heard," Jim said. "How do ye know?"

"Will he be a-goin' to London?"

"Oi expects so. Her Majesty can't do without him, from all Oi hears."

"I thought her had Prince Albert."

"Her has!" Jim replied. "But like all women, her's ready t' have any number o' men on a string."

He spoke casually, then added fiercely:

"Not that Oi wouldn't murder anyone as tried t' hang round ye, and mind ye remembers it!"

"There's no need for you to be jealous," Betsy said. "Will His Grace be staying at Nuneaton House?"

"Where else?" Jim asked. "An' very fine it be, too, as Oi've told ye afore, though there ain't as much room in th' stables as Oi'd like."

Betsy did not reply.

She was thinking, and it required all her concentration to contemplate the extraordinary idea which seemed to have presented itself to her from out of the blue.

* * *

Riding home after seeing the Earl on the Long Gallop, Sorilda thought it a pity that he would not be coming to dinner as her Step-aunt had suggested he might.

She supposed that the invitation had been in the note which she had carried to the stables for Huxley to send to Winsford House.

When Jim had brought back the reply and she had carried it upstairs to her Step-aunt, the Duchess had taken it from her and waited for her to leave the room before she opened it.

"I shall not be allowed to attend the dinner-party," Sorilda told herself.

But she thought she would certainly peep at the Earl from over the bannisters or from the Minstrels' Gallery, which overhung the big Banqueting-Hall that was used when there were guests.

The front of the Minstrels' Gallery was thickly carved and Sorilda had found on previous occasions that it was possible for her to watch the party below without anyone being aware that she was there.

It would be interesting, she thought, to see the Earl at close quarters, but if she had the choice she would rather see his horses.

That night when she was dining with her Uncle and Step-aunt, the Duke said:

"As I am going to London, I might as well take the necklace with me that you want repaired. It will save having to send it up by Courier."

"Are you going to London, Uncle Lionel?" Sorilda asked.

"Yes, I have to see Her Majesty," the Duke replied. "It is a nuisance, as I was at Buckingham Palace only last week. However, I received a letter yesterday morning informing me that Her Majesty was relying on me to support her at a meeting of the Society for the Improvement of the Conditions of the Labouring Classes."

As her Uncle spoke, Sorilda was thinking that before sending the note to the Earl asking him to dinner, the Duchess had known yesterday that he was going to London.

It seemed strange, but she must have known.

Letters arrived early in the morning and were always taken up to the bedrooms before the Duke and Duchess came down to breakfast.

Therefore, if Iris had known that her husband was to be away, what was the point, Sorilda wondered, of inviting the Earl to dinner?

She could hardly expect to give a party on her own.

Then it suddenly struck Sorilda that her Step-aunt might have asked the Earl to dinner with the intention that there should be nobody else there.

That was quite impossible!

However much one could trust the servants, they were human beings, although sometimes people tended to forget the fact, and they would talk, not only inside the Castle but in the village and in the Inn where they drank their ale.

For the Duchess of Nuneaton to dine alone with the Earl of Winsford would be a juicy morsel of gossip which would fly round the County with the speed of a forest-fire.

No, Sorilda told herself; her Step-aunt would be more discreet than to cause a scandal of that sort.

Then why the note?

She found herself thinking of it before she went to bed, after listening to Iris telling her Uncle in dulcet tones which sounded completely sincere that she would miss him desperately and he was to hurry back as soon as possible.

"Now that you are a married man, dearest, the Queen should realise that she cannot rely on you as much as she has done in the past."

"I agree," the Duke replied, "and I can assure you that it is no wish of mine to leave you or to be in London without you."

As if the idea suddenly struck him, he said:

"Why do you not come with me? We could stay an extra night and attend the Opera."

"That would be most enjoyable," the Duchess replied, "but I cannot undertake the journey at such short notice. I am not as mobile as you are, and anyway we shall soon have to be in London for the opening of the Exhibition."

The Duke's face darkened.

"Of course, that is hanging over our heads," he said, "and I could not endure the misery of seeing public money wasted in such an outrageous manner unless you were with me."

"Of course I shall be with you, my dearest husband," the Duchess answered.

The Duke, gratified by her tone, raised her hand to his lips.

After her Uncle had departed early the next morning, with a flurry of last-minute instructions, for-

gotten despatch-cases, and endless consultations over
which coat would be the most suitable for the time of
the year, Sorilda thought it even stranger than she had
done yesterday that her Step-aunt had no wish to accompany him.

The Duchess had moaned over and over again
since they had come down to the country two weeks
ago that she wanted to be in London, for they were
missing Balls and Receptions at which she had every
wish to be present.

Sorilda knew that since she had become a
Duchess, Iris appreciated the fact that every door that
had been closed to her previously was now open, and
as the wife of one of the Premier Dukes of Great
Britain her social position was unassailable.

It must also, Sorilda knew, be frustrating to have
as the viewers of her new gowns only two people—
her husband and her Step-niece—whereas in London
she could listen to the plaudits of a crowd every time
she entered a Ball-Room.

The Duchess found plenty of things for Sorilda
to do during the day, and it was late in the afternoon
before she said:

"We shall dine at seven o'clock tonight as I
wish to retire early. I am in fact feeling somewhat exhausted as there seems to have been so much to do recently."

She certainly did not look tired, Sorilda thought,
and was looking especially lovely with her hair arranged in a new fashion which Harriet had copied
from *The Ladies' Journal*.

They dined downstairs in the small Dining-Room,
and instead of complaining about the food and anything else that came to her notice, as was usual when
she and Sorilda were alone, the Duchess seemed to be
preoccupied by her thoughts.

Sorilda was afraid to speak in case she should
change the trend of them and bring them down retri-
bution on her own head.

As soon as dinner was over the Duchess went up

the stairs towards her *Boudoir,* giving instructions as
she did so to the servants to extinguish unnecessary
lights, as was usual.

This meant, Sorilda knew, that the footmen
would all retire to their own end of the house and
there would only be two old Night-watchmen who
went round regularly once an hour, inspecting the windows and the doors to see that none of them had been
left open.

The Duke and Duchess's rooms were in the west
side of the Castle next to one of two ancient Towers
which flanked either side of what was known as the
"modern part" of the building.

It had in fact been rebuilt two hundred years
ago, and the architect employed at the time had determined to keep it looking as much as possible like
the Castle as it had been originally.

This meant that instead of indulging in large
rooms, they were for the most part small and low, with
arrow-slit windows that did not let in sufficient light.

The Duke's father had, however, made renova-
tions which had improved the facilities considerably.

He had knocked together a number of the small
rooms and made two large bedrooms for himself and
his wife with a *Boudoir* between them. He had created
one large Drawing-Room on the ground floor, which,
like his bedrooms, overlooked the gardens at the back
of the Castle.

This was satisfactory because these rooms faced
south and therefore were filled with sunshine.

Sorilda's bedroom, on the other hand, was over
the front door and looked out onto the Park.

As it looked due-north, virtually no sunshine per-
colated through the two long, narrow windows, and
Sorilda had often thought that she would like to ask
if she could change her bedroom, even if it meant
going up to another floor.

Until the arrival of the Duchess, everything at the
Castle was unchangeable and had to be as it had
always been.

Sorilda had therefore continued to sleep in the room she had occupied when she had first come to the Castle after her father and mother's death, and she imagined that if she asked for any change now, the Duchess would feel justified in putting her in the servants' quarters.

Worse still, the alternative might be a part of the Castle that was even colder than her present room, which could literally be freezing in the winter months.

It was a relief to know that tonight at any rate it was warm enough to have the windows open, and also to see lying on the small table by the windows a book that she was looking forward to reading.

Although her Tutors had been taken away from her, the Duke's Comptroller had not revealed to her Step-aunt that he purchased for Sorilda any book she wished to own.

As he was mostly in London, where in his office in Nuneaton House he looked after the whole of the Duke's properties as well as dealing with his private correspondence, Sorilda had got into the way of writing almost weekly to Mr. Burnham.

He was always so prompt in supplying anything she asked for that she thought perhaps he understood what she was suffering since her Uncle's marriage.

He certainly must have thought it strange how often he was told to replace servants at the Castle, because in the past, those who were employed there came when they were young and left only when they died.

Sorilda undressed and put on her dressing-gown before she opened the book.

She had no intention of going to bed, because it was far more comfortable to sit in an arm-chair by the window, put her feet on a stool, and read first in the fading light of the sunset, then later by the light of several candles.

The Duke had installed gas-lighting in some parts of the Castle, but the only bedrooms to have it were his own and the Duchess's, and as it had been installed before Sorilda's arrival, there was no question of her being accorded such a privilege.

She did not mind. Actually she preferred the candles, thinking that when those on the chandeliers and the sconces were lit, they gave the Castle a romantic atmosphere that was sadly lacking at other times.

To make sure she was really comfortable, Sorilda took a pillow from the bed and placed it on the chair behind her, then opened her book, leant back, and prepared to enjoy herself.

Yet somehow the words did not grip her as she had expected them to do.

Instead, she found herself looking out the window, seeing the sky change from the crimson and gold of the sunset to the first sable of the night.

"It will be a fine day tomorrow," she told herself, remembering the old adage: "Red sky at night, shepherds' delight."

That meant that she would be able to ride at six o'clock, and she thought she would once again go to the Burnt Oak and watch the Earl on one of his superb horses.

Sorilda had loved riding ever since she was a child, and because her father enjoyed hunting they had always had a stable full of first-class hunters, even though her mother had complained that so much was spent on them that she and Sorilda would have to go bare-foot.

Sorilda found it a joy to ride with her father, and often as she grew older they would go on long expeditions.

While they returned home slowly, because the horses were tired, he would talk to her and she would learn more from him in the hours they spent together than she would from a thousand books or a dozen erudite Tutors.

"Papa would have admired the Earl's horses," Sorilda told herself.

She only wished that she knew more about them. She would have liked to know, for instance, what was the breeding of the horse the Earl had been riding yesterday morning.

She would also think it interesting to know what he paid for them, and she suspected that that question could be answered by Huxley.

He was an inveterate gossip and always knew what was taking place in other stables in the County.

"I am quite certain he finds the Earl's horses more interesting than anybody else's, because he is jealous of them, just as Uncle Edmund is jealous of the Earl himself."

The idea was amusing, then as she looked out onto the deepening shadows beneath the great trees in the Park, she saw far in the distance someone riding in the direction of the Castle.

She wondered who it could be, because at this time of night she knew it would not be anyone from their own stables.

She thought that perhaps it was a groom coming with a message, but even so it was late when in the country people kept such early hours.

She could see the horse and rider moving amongst the trees and it suddenly struck her that there was something vaguely familiar about them both.

She watched, sitting up straight in her chair to see more clearly.

Whoever it was, he was not coming directly to the house but moving across her line of vision and then, she thought, turning almost as if he intended to approach the Castle from a different angle.

Because she was curious, she stood up and leant out the window.

Now she could see much more clearly, and as the Castle was built on an incline she could see for a long distance, and despite the gathering shadows and the darkening sky, she was aware that the rider was approaching the Castle from the west side.

'How strange!' Sorilda thought. 'And why the west side? The stables are on the east.'

She craned her neck a little farther to watch him, then as he drew nearer it struck her that she knew who the rider and the horse were.

"It is impossible! I am being absurd!" she told herself. "There are other men in the world, so why should I think of him?"

Then she was sure, completely sure, that it was the Earl of Winsford who was riding towards the Castle.

Then she understood, and everything that had puzzled her as regarded her Step-aunt's note fell into place.

Now that her Uncle was away, the Earl was visiting Iris!

For a moment it seemed to Sorilda so incredible that she could hardly believe the whole idea was not just a figment of her imagination.

Then she knew it was not a fantasy but something that was actually happening.

Her Step-aunt had known that the Duke was going to London and had conveyed the information to the Earl, pretending for Sorilda's benefit that she was inviting him to a dinner-party.

The note that Jim had brought back, which had been given to her by one of the footmen and which she had passed to her Step-aunt, had been his acceptance.

Now, incredible though it seemed, he was calling at nine o'clock at night.

But how could he possibly do so without the servants being aware of it?

Even as her mind asked the question, Sorilda knew the answer.

When she had first come to the Castle she had been very intrigued by the two high Towers which were all that remained of the original Norman building.

The twisting staircases inside them, the tiny rooms, and the arrow-slit windows had encouraged her to visit them not once but dozens of times, because they seemed to her redolent of all the romanticism of the Knights and the Lordly Barons who had once ruled England.

The staircase in the West Tower had a door opening into the Duke's bedroom, and though the door was kept bolted on the inside, her Uncle had once said to her with a laugh:

"If ever I wish to leave the Castle unnoticed, I can go down this staircase, which, as you see, passes my own bedroom."

"It would be very useful, Uncle Edmund, if you were a Royalist escaping from the Cromwellian troops," Sorilda had remarked.

"I believe something like that did happen somewhere in our history," the Duke replied. "You must ask Mr. Burnham to give you a catalogue of the books which are in the Library."

Sorilda had searched through the history of the family, but she had found nothing about an Eaton having been persecuted at that time.

Earlier there had been many battles which had raged round the Castle, and at one time a siege had brought its inhabitants almost to the verge of starvation.

Because it was part of her own history and her father had told her so much about the Eatons and the way they had served their country, Sorilda had tried to love the Castle and be proud of everything it stood for.

But since her Step-aunt had come to live there she had found it very difficult.

Now she knew that she was shocked—shocked to the point where she was horrified—to think that a woman who had become a member of the family and was the Duchess of Nuneaton should deceive her husband and behave in a manner that Sorilda's mother would have thought reprehensible even in a woman of the village.

'Uncle Edmund loves her,' Sorilda thought, 'and it is a betrayal of him and of the whole family that she should break her marriage-vows six months after she made them!'

Now she could no longer see the horse or the rider, but she knew that they would be passing through the shrubbery which was planted on the west side of the house, where the bushes, high and concealing because they had been there for so long, reached right up to the door of the Tower.

There were plenty of places for the Earl to tie up his horse, and doubtless Iris would already have opened the door at the bottom of the Tower and the one into the Duke's bedroom.

"It is disgraceful of him!" Sorilda exclaimed. "He is a gentleman and a neighbour. Although Uncle Edmund does not like him, that is no reason for him to behave so abominably."

She thought that the Earl, who not only looked handsome but had a presence that was unmistakable, should not stoop to deceive someone like her Uncle.

She supposed that in a way she was disappointed in him.

But now she remembered that she had heard Huxley and the other grooms saying things that she had not noticed particularly at the time, but which might have told her, had she been interested, that the Earl was very much a "ladies' man."

They had, of course, been careful what they said in front of her, for they still thought of her as a child.

But the innuendoes had been there and she could remember similar suggestions put in a more refined way by the guests who had sat round her Uncle's table.

"I hear Winsford is making quite a name for himself in London," she now recalled hearing one old gentleman say at dinner.

"In what way?" the Duke had asked somewhat coldly.

"He has an eye both for a horse and for a pretty woman," the gentleman had boomed, speaking unnecessarily loudly because he was deaf.

The Duke had looked down his nose and the ladies at the table had pretended to blush.

"Come on, Your Grace," the gentleman had said. "Do not pretend to be surprised. You were a bit of a dog yourself in your youth!"

Her Uncle, Sorilda remembered, had seemed rather pleased at the compliment.

"That is not surprising, my dear Duke," the gentleman's wife had said, patting him on the arm with her fan. "You were always the most handsome man that ever graced the Hunt Ball, and I remember all too well how we girls always prayed that you would ask us to dance."

"And that is what the girls of today are doing," the gentleman said, "only now they are praying that young Winsford will notice them. A large number, I understand, have had their prayers answered!"

He laughed at his own joke until he choked, and when he had been patted on the back and made to drink some water, the conversation changed to another subject.

In the back of Sorilda's mind she had thought that the Earl was as successful with women as he was in breeding horses, only somehow she had not expected him to pursue somebody like her Step-aunt into the very precincts of the Nuneaton stronghold.

"It is disgraceful!" Sorilda said again, and opened her book determinedly.

* * *

As it happened, the Earl of Winsford had been surprised when the previous day the Duchess's note had been brought to him.

He had just been about to leave the house to ride round the estate with one of his friends, Peter Lansdown.

As he disliked keeping the horses waiting, he

had opened the note impatiently, not bothering even to glance at the writing or guess from whom it had come.

When he had read what the Duchess had written he had stood still for a moment, as if it both surprised and intrigued him.

"What is it, Sholto?" Peter Lansdown enquired. "If you are going to cancel our ride I shall be extremely annoyed! It is my last chance of trying out your superb horses, as I have to leave exceedingly early tomorrow morning."

"That means I shall be alone," the Earl said.

"I am sure there are plenty of people to join you, if that is what you desire," his friend replied, a note of amusement in his voice.

The Earl, however, appeared not to be listening.

Instead he seemed to be debating something with himself and his friend thought he was obviously considering what he should do.

Then with a smile that had something mischievous about it, he said:

"Ride ahead of me down the drive, Peter. I will not be a moment, but I have to answer an invitation."

As he spoke he hurried from the Hall, scribbled a reply to the Duchess's note, and came back only a minute or so later to hand it to his Major Domo.

"Send this to Nuneaton Castle."

"The groom who brought the note is waiting, My Lord."

"Then give it to him."

As the Earl spoke he walked swiftly across the Hall and down the steps to where his horse was waiting.

He mounted and rode after his friend, who had only reached the bridge that spanned the lake.

"Have you made a momentous decision?" Peter Lansdown asked as the Earl joined him.

They had been friends for many years, had served in the same Regiment, and had both supported

Prince Albert whole-heartedly in his desire to marry Art with Commerce and show the world an Exhibition of Culture that would astound the whole country.

Peter Lansdown was a Member of Parliament and his voice in the House had continually put the Prince's point of view to those who had been hostile from its very inception.

"I have just received an invitation which has surprised me," the Earl admitted as they rode side-by-side.

"I should have thought you were too old and certainly too experienced to be surprised by anything a woman might suggest," Peter Lansdown replied, laughing.

"How do you know it was a woman?" the Earl enquired.

"That was obvious from the expression on your face," his friend answered, "and I would also wager one hundred to one that you accepted the proposition in question."

"That was your fault."

"Why?"

"Because you are leaving me alone, and quite frankly, Peter, like most Englishmen, I dislike eating by myself."

"I have already told you that is unnecessary where you are concerned. But if you dislike it happening even occasionally, there is one very easy remedy."

"What is that?" the Earl asked.

He was only giving his friend half his attention and it was obvious that his mind was elsewhere.

"You could get married!"

"Good God, it is not a case of melancholy!" the Earl exclaimed. "And incidentally, marriage is something I have no wish for now or at any time!"

"You cannot be serious?"

"I am very serious. Marriage, my dear Peter, is not for me! I am a born bachelor! To be tied to one woman, however attractive, would make me feel as if

I were imprisoned in a dungeon from which there was no escape."

Peter Lansdown laughed. Then he said:

"I had no idea that you felt so strongly on the subject, although I was well aware that you have been extremely skilful in eluding the bait that has been dangled over your nose ever since you were eighteen!"

They had reached the top of the drive, and as they turned towards the Long Gallop, Peter Lansdown drew in his horse to look back at the house.

It was lying a little below them and with its background of green trees it looked overwhelmingly magnificent in the spring sunshine.

"Admiring my possession?" the Earl asked.

"I was just thinking that sooner or later you will have to change your mind and at least produce an heir," Peter Lansdown replied. "You know as well as I do that your Cousin Hubert is not the right type of character to wear your coronet with dignity!"

They both laughed, the Earl somewhat wryly.

His heir presumptive was a young man who had refused all social responsibility and instead spent most of his time in Paris, painting excruciatingly bad pictures and enjoying himself exuberantly with the women who patronised the night-life of the French Capital.

He had grown a beard, wore the velvet coat of the artist, a huge floppy tie, and, when he remembered, a beret on the side of his head.

"I simply cannot imagine Hubert at Winsford," Peter Lansdown said, "so stop talking nonsense, Sholto, and make up your mind that in the next ten years or so you will have, for the sake of the family, to embrace the bonds of holy matrimony."

"I am damned if I will!" the Earl retorted. "I enjoy life as I am, and as I have said, any woman I married would soon become such a crashing bore that I should find myself murdering her!"

"Beget your heir first!" Peter Lansdown said. "Then you can drop her in the lake or push her off the roof and nobody will be in the least concerned!"

The Earl threw back his head and laughed.

"Peter, you are incredible! If I listened to you I should become not only a criminal but a murderer, and that would certainly not embellish the family escutcheon!"

"Remember that I am very willing to help you," Peter Lansdown said. "In the meantime, enjoy yourself."

"That is exactly what I intend to do," the Earl replied. "Why should I say no to any rich peach which is ready to fall into my lap?"

As he spoke, he thought that that was a very good description of Iris.

She was exactly like a peach in her softness and in the way she managed with her fair hair and pale blue eyes to have a kind of bloom on her that other women lacked.

The Earl had in fact admitted to himself that he had been quite disappointed—or was the right word "piqued"?—when so soon after they had met she had accepted the Duke of Nuneaton and had become a bride before he could get his hands on her for the second time.

They had been introduced at a house-party given by one of the Earl's more dashing friends for the St. Leger Race-Meeting, which took place in Yorkshire.

The moment the Earl had walked into his friend's house, having just broken the driving-record from London, he had seen Iris and known that it had been worth the effort to come so far.

However, the house-party was surprisingly respectable because the host had been obliged at the last moment to find accommodation for his mother, who unpredictably had wished to attend the Race-Meeting.

This rather constricted the behaviour of the other guests, who were used to being very free and easy in that particular house for these particular races.

It was therefore not on the first night but the

second that the Earl, as he knew was expected of him, found his way to Iris's bedroom.

With his vast experience of women and his expertise which had gained him the reputation of being the best lover in London, the Earl had sensed that beneath Iris's angelic appearance lurked the burning fires of a passionate woman.

He had not been disappointed, and he had felt when he returned to his bedroom as dawn broke that it had been an enjoyable if predictable night.

The following day he had left after the racing, and while he looked forward to seeing Iris again in London, when he had opened *The Times* on his return it was to find that her marriage to the Duke of Nuneaton had already taken place.

He had a feeling that that was not the end of the story, and when he had danced with her at the State Ball he had known that marriage had not damped down the fires which raged within her.

At the same time, he had hesitated before deliberately assisting his neighbour's wife to infidelity.

One of the Earl's principles had always been not to make love to a woman in her husband's house when he was to all intents and purposes a friend.

Yet it would have been impossible in the country for Iris to come to him without her servants being aware of it.

He knew that in consequence he had either to refuse her invitation or throw his principles overboard.

He remembered that the Duke had never liked him and had often gone out of his way to make him feel that he took very much second-place in County affairs when he was present.

What was more, he resented the Duke's attitude over Prince Albert's building of the Crystal Palace.

To the Earl it seemed simple loyalty on the part of those who were frequently at Buckingham Palace, and who were trusted both by the Queen and her Consort, to support the Prince in the project which could do nothing but good for the country and might conceivably improve foreign relations with the whole world.

It was perhaps this thought more than anything else which made the Earl decide that if the Duke could not look after his own wife it was not for him to teach him his business.

What was more, he thought, it would certainly be a pleasure to see Iris again and to find the fire burning fiercely on those softly curved lips which looked as if they never uttered anything more arousing than a prayer or a psalm.

Only as he rode through the twilight towards the Castle did the Earl ask if he was making a fool of himself and taking unnecessary risks in pursuit of a woman whose favours he had already enjoyed.

As he reached the boundary between the two estates he very nearly turned back.

He had the uncomfortable feeling that he was inviting danger, although why he should feel like that he had no idea.

"I must be getting old if I cannot embark on an ordinary adventure without soul-searching," he told himself scornfully, "and God knows I am too young to enjoy sitting alone and listening to my conscience!"

He crossed onto the Duke's land and told himself that ten years ago, when he first came down from Oxford, he would have thought this was a thrill that could not possibly be missed.

He could only find himself hoping as he rode on that Iris after all would be worth the trouble he was taking over her.

The Earl had often found in his love-affairs that the expectation and indeed the thrill of a first encounter could never be equalled on subsequent occasions.

Indeed, in his experience it was fatal to revive a love-affair that had once seemed over. However, that was not true in Iris's case, because one fiery night could hardly constitute a love-affair.

And yet, he told himself, he might have done

better to leave well enough alone, and when it came down to it, he had no desire to upset the Duke, which it would undoubtedly do if he had the least idea of what was happening.

Then he told himself that Iris would certainly know on which side her bread was buttered.

He had made it very clear to her, as he had made it to all women, that he was a lover, not a husband, and that his intentions were strictly dishonourable and nothing and nobody could change him.

'She is certainly old enough to look after herself,' the Earl excused himself, 'and there is no reason why I should play nurse-maid.'

He had reached the side of the West Tower and found as he rode through the bushes that there were plenty of stalwart boughs on which to tie the reins of his horse.

Having dismounted, he saw the door of the Tower just ahead of him and as he drew nearer he realised that it was slightly ajar.

The sky overhead was now almost dark and the first evening star was twinkling above the top of the Tower.

The Earl looked up and, seeing the arrow-slit windows, thought that in earlier times doubtless by now he would be lying on the ground with an arrow in his chest.

Then with a smile on his lips he mocked at his own fancy, and, pushing open the heavy oak door, started to climb up the twisting stone steps towards a gleaming light.

Chapter Three

Sorilda realised that she was feeling cold.

When she had lit the candles to go on reading she had drawn the curtains to keep out the moths but had left the window open.

Now there was a night breeze moving the curtains and she felt it penetrating through her thin dressing-gown, although not until this moment had she felt the chill of it.

She rose to her feet, realising as she did so that, although she had forced herself to try to concentrate on her book, one part of her brain was continually occupied with the Duchess and the Earl.

She told herself that it was really ridiculous to be so shocked, and yet she knew that the way they were behaving offended not only her sense of propriety but also her instinct for everything that was beautiful.

It had continually surprised her that her Step-aunt, who was so exquisitely lovely, should have such an unpleasant character, but she had never for one moment suspected that she was immoral as well.

It was, she thought, like finding a canker in what appeared to be a perfect fruit or an earwig in the heart of a lily.

"I will not think about it," Sorilda told herself determinedly.

She went to the dressing-table and took the pins from her hair, knowing as it fell over her shoulders that it was greasy from the pomade that Harriet had applied to it, and hating her Step-aunt because she was determined to make her look as unattractive as she could.

Once a week Sorilda washed her hair, and when she did so it was a joy to see the red-gold of it falling in soft waves against her white skin.

It always reminded her of her mother, and she thought how appalled she would have been to see the mess and ugliness of the hair she had brushed with such pride ever since Sorilda had been a small child.

Now, because it gave her something to do, she brushed out her long tresses, feeling it becoming more buoyant with every stroke until it fell over her shoulders in a cloud of red glory.

It was still dank and limp on top of her head, and because she disliked this so much, she rubbed it with a towel until much of the grease was removed and she could see it glinting in the candlelight when she looked in the mirror.

As she stared at her reflection she knew that in the morning Harriet would come to apply more of the pomade and to skin it back into a hard bun at the back of her head which was often so tight that it hurt her.

She had given up protesting because it only meant that her Step-aunt would rant and rave at her and she would feel humiliated because she was so helpless and there was nothing she could do about it.

Now as she thought of the disgraceful way in which the Duchess was behaving, Sorilda felt that it would have an effect on the very atmosphere of the Castle.

Then she told herself that that was an exaggeration. The Castle had survived, just as the Eaton family had, despite crimes of every sort and description, and there must have been Duchesses in the past who had behaved as badly as if not worse than Iris.

Admittedly, if there had been, there was no record of them, and perhaps they had been clever enough to get away with it, as undoubtedly the new Duchess would do.

Sorilda took off her dressing-gown and was just about to get into bed when she was suddenly aware of an unexpected noise.

For a moment she could not think what it was. Then as it continued she went to the window and drew aside the curtains to look out.

To her astonishment she saw the lights of a carriage in the darkness beneath the trees which bordered the drive.

It was difficult at the moment to see anything else until as the trees ended at the bottom of the incline which led to the Castle, she saw a man on horseback ride away from the side of the carriage in the direction of the West Tower.

As he did so, Sorilda knew that the carriage was the one in which her Uncle had left for London, accompanied, as was usual on such a journey, by two outriders.

For a moment she thought she must be mistaken.

He had left only this morning, and if he had returned so soon he must have come back immediately on reaching Nuneaton House.

Perhaps, she thought, he had forgotten something important and sent the carriage back to collect it, in which case one of the senior servants would have to be awakened to find it for him.

The carriage reached the courtyard and now Sorilda knew that there was no mistake. Rowlandson, the elderly coachman, was on the box, and beside him was James, the footman who also valeted her Uncle when he left home for a short visit.

There was only one outrider now to draw the horse to a standstill as at the same time the carriage stopped beneath the steps.

James jumped down from the box and opened

the door, and looking down Sorilda saw her Uncle step out.

He had returned!

Now with a feeling of horror she realised what he would find when he entered the house.

For one second it passed through her mind that it would serve her Step-aunt right and it was only justice that she should be punished for her behaviour.

Then she knew what a terrible blow it would be for her Uncle.

He loved his new wife with a depth of emotion that Sorilda had never thought him capable of feeling, and as she was well aware, he was already exceedingly jealous.

Whatever she might feel personally about Iris, her Uncle in his own way had never shown her anything but kindness and she knew that if she could save him from knowing of his wife's infidelity she must do so.

Below her, James was tugging at the bell which stood beside the iron-studded oak door. Then he raised the knocker to make a sound which Sorilda knew would bring the Night-watchmen hurrying to the Hall.

Without waiting another second, she ran across the room, pulled open the door, and sped across the corridor.

The door to the Duchess's bedroom was on the other side and a little to the right, and as she knocked she thought she heard the murmur of voices.

If there had been anyone talking they were hushed into silence, and Sorilda knocked again.

Because she felt that her Step-aunt was deliberately pretending to be asleep, she said as loudly as she dared:

"Uncle Edmund has just returned home!"

She thought for a moment that no-one had heard her, then there was a cry that was almost a shriek.

Because she felt she had done what she could and had no wish for her Uncle to see her in the passage,

Sorilda hurried back to her own room, shut the door, and got into bed.

She did not lie down but sat up with her back against the pillows, her whole body tense as she listened.

Because her bedroom was just above the front door and voices echoed in the Castle, she could hear the murmur of what she thought must be the Nightwatchmen.

Then, because her every nerve was strained, she was sure that she could hear her Uncle's footsteps coming up the stairs even before they were actually within earshot.

Being such a large man and stoutly built, his footsteps were heavy, and there was no doubt that she could hear them when he stepped from the top of the stairs onto the wide corridor where the polished boards were not carpeted but covered with Persian rugs.

Now the footsteps were menacingly loud, and as Sorilda heard them coming down the corridor the door of her bedroom opened and someone stepped inside.

For a moment she thought she must be dreaming as she saw the Earl coming into the room, and as he shut the door quietly behind him, she watched him in astonishment before he turned his face towards her.

He was wearing a shirt and long, tight-fitting trousers and over his arm he carried his coat and a black cravat.

As if he was surprised to see her, the Earl stood very still. Then as they stared at each other Sorilda said almost beneath her breath:

"You should not ... come here! You must ... leave by the West Tower!"

"I tried to," the Earl replied in a voice as low as hers, "but there was someone coming up the stairs."

With a start Sorilda remembered the outrider she had seen moving in the direction of the Tower.

He would have found the Earl's horse, she

thought, and then on her Uncle's instructions would have climbed the stairs to his bedroom.

"I apologise for my intrusion," the Earl said, still in a very low voice, "but I saw the light under your door and had no time to look elsewhere."

As he spoke, Sorilda remembered that when she had crossed the corridor to knock on her Step-aunt's bedroom door, the candles had been extinguished and the only light to guide her came from the candles in her own bedroom.

Now she thought that with any luck her Uncle would not have seen the Earl and he would manage to escape detection.

Even as she thought of it she heard the Duke's footsteps pass her door and a second later there was the sound of another door opening. Then quite audibly there was her Step-aunt's voice crying:

"Edmund! What a surprise! Why have you returned?"

"Where is he?"

The Duke shouted the words, and there was no doubt, Sorilda thought, that he was in a towering rage.

"Where is—who?"

"You know perfectly well who I am talking about!" the Duke stormed. "And when I find him I will throw both of you out of the house if I do not kill you before I do so!"

There was a shriek from the Duchess as if in fear, then she said:

"What are you talking about? What do you mean? I do not understand!"

There was no answer from the Duke, but there was a noise as if he was opening cupboards and wardrobes and, finding nothing inside, slamming them shut behind him.

Then they heard his footsteps receding and Sorilda knew that he was walking into the *Boudoir* and towards his own bedroom.

She looked at the Earl, her eyes very wide, and saw that while she had been listening to her Uncle he had put on his coat and tied his tie so that now he was fully dressed and very elegant.

It flashed through Sorilda's mind that as he was so handsome there was some excuse for Iris in preferring him to her ageing husband.

Then she told herself quickly that she despised them both and their behaviour shocked and revolted her.

She looked away from the Earl and, listening again, thought she heard the murmur of voices in the distance.

"The groom whom you heard climbing the West Tower," she said in a whisper, "will have seen your horse."

"I am aware of that," the Earl replied.

Sorilda thought he was snubbing her and she told herself that had it not been for her intervention, the Duke would have discovered him in her Step-aunt's bedroom.

"How am I going to get out of here?" the Earl asked, and again she thought his tone was ungracious.

"If you look out the window," she said, "you can see if the carriage has moved away. In which case, if you avoid the Night-watchmen, you might be able to leave by the front door."

"I should think that is unlikely."

As he spoke the Earl walked to the window and flung aside the curtain to look out.

Even as he did so, the door of Sorilda's bedroom opened and the Duke stood there.

For a moment it seemed that his eyes moved to take in every detail: Sorilda sitting up in bed with her red hair falling over her nightgown, the Earl with his hand on the curtain, his face turned towards the door at the first sound of it opening.

"So you are here!"

The Duke's voice seemed to ring out and for a moment the Earl had no answer and Sorilda could only hold her breath.

Then there was a sudden cry from the door as

the Duchess stepped into the room wearing, Sorilda noticed, a most attractive dressing-gown of blue velvet trimmed with real lace.

For a moment she seemed to stare wide-eyed as the Duke had done at the Earl and Sorilda, before she threw up her hands and exclaimed:

"Sorilda! How could you! You wicked girl! How could I have guessed—how could I have known—that you would behave in such an outrageous manner!"

For a moment Sorilda did not understand. Then she realised with a little gasp that everyone in the room was looking at her.

Before she could speak, the Duchess said to the Duke:

"I am appalled, Edmund! Absolutely appalled that this should have happened! And when you were away from home! It is hard to believe the evidence of my own eyes!"

The Duke had a look of anger on his face together with an expression of suspicion that made him look with narrowed eyes first at his wife, then at the Earl.

Slowly, as if he chose his words, he said:

"I cannot believe that my niece invited you here, My Lord. Unless my memory fails me, you have not even met her."

"Then you must have been mistaken, Edmund," the Duchess said quickly, "and now that I think of it, I remember someone in the house—I think it was Harriet—told me that Sorilda sent a note to Winsford Park yesterday and received a reply."

The Duke opened his lips to speak, but before he could do so, the Duchess went on:

"That is how she must have made the assignation."

She looked at the Earl and said:

"I feel sure, My Lord, that you can assure my husband in all truth that you have not received a letter signed by me in the last forty-eight hours."

There was just a twist to the Earl's lips as he

spoke for the first time since the Duke and Duchess had entered the room.

"That is true."

Sorilda thought at once that he was lying. Then it struck her that perhaps the note which her Step-aunt had sent him had in fact been unsigned, in which case it would be even more difficult to prove her innocence.

As she remembered how Iris had sent her to the stables with a note for the Earl and how she had received the reply, she was astute enough to realise that her Step-aunt, with considerable cleverness, was building up a case against her.

With an effort she found her voice and said:

"Uncle ... Edmund ... I would like to ... tell you ..."

Before she could proceed further, the Duchess gave a little scream and, walking towards her, said:

"We will not listen to your lies! Nor shall you make things worse than they are already! I am ashamed of you, bitterly ashamed! I shall see that your Uncle punishes you as you richly deserve!"

Her voice was vindictive but, Sorilda thought, also apprehensive.

Then in the light from the candles beside her bed, she could see that that was the truth.

Iris was indeed afraid, and she was fighting with every weapon in her power for her own survival.

The Earl walked towards the Duke.

"I must ask Your Grace," he said, "to accept my apologies for this exceedingly unpleasant scene. Perhaps I could call on Your Grace tomorrow morning at your convenience, and I am perfectly prepared to apologise further."

"And you think that will satisfy me?" the Duke asked.

"I can only hope so," the Earl replied.

It seemed as if the two men were fencing with each other warily, both acutely aware of the gravity and impact of the battle between them.

"I think very little you could say would satisfy me, Winsford," the Duke said after a moment. "I was informed that in my absence you were visiting my wife."

"Who could have said such a thing? Who could have maligned me in such a manner?" the Duchess interrupted. "Was it an anonymous letter, and if so, how could you have been so foolish as to believe it? I love you, Edmund! You are all the world to me! How can you imagine for one moment that I would be unfaithful with another man?"

"My informant was very precise in his accusations," the Duke said coldly. "I was told that the Earl would enter the house by the West Tower, which he undoubtedly did, as his horse is there waiting for him, and that you would be waiting for him with 'longing'!"

His voice seemed to linger on the last word, and Sorilda, listening to him, thought that her Step-aunt went even paler than she was already, and she knew that her Uncle must be quoting from the actual note.

"You tell me," the Duke went on, "that I was misinformed, and in the time it takes for me to enter the house and climb the stairs, I find Winsford not in your room but in my niece's."

He glanced towards the window as he spoke.

The Earl had pulled aside the curtain and as he looked out the Duke could see that the window was open.

"Strange, Winsford," he said, "that you did not hear me arrive, seeing that this room faces the front of the house. You might have had time, might you not, to find a different hiding-place from where I discovered you?"

Sorilda felt a little of her tension relaxing.

Her Uncle had not believed her Step-aunt's accusation against her and now she would no longer be embroiled.

For a moment she felt so relieved that she leant back against the pillows.

Then the Duke continued as if he was choosing his words:

"At the same time, if my wife, as she says is not involved, then I must of course defend the honour of my niece, since, following the death of her parents, I am her Guardian."

Sorilda straightened her back again. She wondered what this had to do with it.

"I must therefore," the Duke went on, "request that you make recompense in the only possible way."

As he spoke, Sorilda was aware that the Earl had stiffened, and the Duchess, looking from one man to the other, asked:

"What are you talking about? What are you saying, Edmund?"

"I am making it clear," the Duke replied in a steely voice, "that the only honourable thing the Earl of Winsford can do in the circumstances is to offer my niece marriage."

"Marriage?" The exclamation was a shriek. "You cannot expect that?"

"Why not?" the Duke enquired. "Surely, my dear, you must realise how deep his affection must be for Sorilda if he rides at night from his house to mine, enters it in a secretive manner which of course she must have contrived, and is found in her bedroom when she is actually in bed wearing only a nightgown."

The Duke's tone was scathing and now Sorilda exclaimed:

"Please ... Uncle Edmund ... you must ... listen to me."

The Duke looked towards her and so did both the Duchess and the Earl.

Three pairs of eyes seemed to be waiting for her statement: one pair suspicious, the other two apprehensive.

'I shall tell the truth,' Sorilda thought.

But then she realised, almost as if a voice were telling her aloud, that here was the escape she had prayed for.

Instead of long years incarcerated in a prison in which she was subjected to the insults and cruelty of her Step-aunt, she could expect a very different life.

It might be frightening and also humiliating to be married to a man who did not want her and whom she despised.

But anything would be better than being bullied and crushed into insignificance by Iris.

For six months she had forced her will upon her to the point, Sorilda thought, where she had known that there was no appeal, no way that she would ever know anything different from the dreary round of unpalatable tasks and being thrust farther and farther into the background and allowed to meet no-one from outside the Castle.

This was her chance.

It might seem a strange and desperate one. It might, as she had already thought, be more frightening than anything she had ever encountered in her life before, but at least she would be free of the Duchess, and nothing else at the moment seemed to be of any importance.

Six eyes were watching her. Three people were waiting to hear what she had to say, and now, a little lamely because she had to change her words and had no time to think, she said:

"I am . . . sorry . . . Uncle Edmund . . . I am . . . desperately sorry. I can only . . . beg of you to . . . forgive me."

Just for a moment there was a look of puzzlement in the Duke's eyes.

Then as he looked quickly at his wife and saw the relief on her face that she was unable to hide, the lines of cynicism seemed to deepen on his face as he turned again to the Earl.

"I am still waiting, Winsford."

The Earl straightened his shoulders, almost as if he were a soldier marching towards certain death, before he said:

"I can only request Your Grace's permission to pay my addresses to your niece."

"I will not only permit you to do so," the Duke

replied, "but to make certain that you make an honest woman of her, I suggest that your marriage should take place as soon as you procure a Special License."

There was a little pause before he added:

"That should take approximately forty-eight hours, and as today is Wednesday I suggest that the ceremony will be solemnized here in the Castle at noon on Friday."

"This is ridiculous!" the Duchess exclaimed. "Why the unnecessary hurry? Surely it would be best to think everything over and not to act in such precipitate haste?"

"I am of course thinking of Sorilda," the Duke replied.

His voice was sarcastic as he went on:

"There could be unfortunate consequences of this secret liaison, which may of course have entailed a long chain of clandestine meetings, in which case you will understand, my dear, that the sooner she is legally his wife, the better!"

Sorilda thought the Earl was about to speak, but before he could do so, the Duke stood back and opened wide the door behind him.

"Good-night, My Lord!" he said. "I will make all arrangements with my private Chaplain for the marriage and will expect Your Lordship here a few minutes before noon on Friday, with, of course, the Special Licence."

The Earl inclined his head.

Then as if he did not trust his voice, he went from the room and Sorilda heard him walking down the passage towards the stairs.

It seemed as if it took a few minutes for the Duchess to find her voice. Then she said in a tone which told Sorilda that she was very angry:

"Really, Edmund! I think you are being ridiculous over this. I grant you Sorilda has been extremely indiscreet, but perhaps she has no wish to marry the Earl, nor he her."

"In which case," the Duke replied, "it is even

more reprehensible that they should arrange an assignation in her bedroom."

The Duchess made an exasperated little sound and the Duke continued:

"As I can hardly allow my niece to behave as if she were a prostitute or the Earl to walk in and out of the Castle as if it were a brothel, I will take rigorous steps to see that this sort of thing does not happen again!"

He was looking at the Duchess in a manner which told Sorilda that she could not possibly misunderstand the message he was conveying to her.

For a moment she thought her Step-aunt was going to argue, but the Duke went on:

"There is one other alternative, of course—I could turn Sorilda out, bag and baggage, to fend for herself. That might be, in some people's point of view, the right punishment for such behaviour. Or should I call it a crime? But I feel that you of all people would wish me to be more merciful."

Now the Duchess understood quite clearly that she was being threatened, and it seemed to Sorilda, as she watched and listened, that she shrank physically and seemed to grow smaller.

"I would not wish you to be—cruel, Edmund," she said at length in a voice that trembled.

"That is what I thought," the Duke replied, "and now let us retire, for I am tired after so much travelling, and it is very pleasant to know that you, my dear wife, are so glad to welcome me home!"

The sarcasm in the Duke's voice was unmistakable and with a sound that might have been a sob the Duchess turned and walked from the room.

The Duke followed her and only when he reached the door to stand for a moment looking back at Sorilda did he seem to take in the way in which her red hair glinted in the candlelight and the fear in her large eyes.

Then he said quietly, as if he did not wish his wife to hear:

"For a husband you might do worse than the Earl of Winsford!"

The door shut behind him and now Sorilda put her hands up to her face.

What had she done? What had happened?

It seemed impossible that so much had occurred within what could not have been more than ten or fifteen minutes, and yet because of it her whole life had changed.

She looked back, wondering what she could have said to exonerate herself without completely destroying the Duchess, or, if she had not been able to do that, without entering into a long and vitriolic argument in which, as her Step-aunt had covered her tracks so cleverly, it would have been hard to prove herself innocent.

Her Uncle knew the truth, there was no doubt about that. He had not been deceived by the Earl being found in her bedroom or by the play-acting of the Duchess.

He had been sharp-witted enough to realise that if the arrival of his carriage had alerted her, it was she who had given the Earl time to move from the Duchess's room into hers.

Whoever had told him the contents of the note that the Duchess had sent the Earl obviously had also conveyed that he would enter the house by the West Tower.

No, the Duke had realised the truth, Sorilda thought, and as she went over and over in her mind exactly what had been done and said, she knew that whatever protestations she could have made, the result would inevitably have been the same.

"For a husband you might do worse than the Earl of Winsford!"

Her Uncle's last comment seemed to ring in her ears, and she asked herself how could she marry a man, however handsome he might be, or however proficient a horseman, when she despised him utterly.

Despite her extensive reading, Sorilda was very

innocent and had little real knowledge of the way people behaved.

Scandal had very seldom been talked of when she was at home with her father and mother, for the simple reason that it bored them both and they had so many other subjects in which they were interested.

Sorilda therefore had really very little idea that in the Social World it was common for gentlemen like the Earl to have a long series of *affaires de coeur* with beautiful women who did not consider it immoral to be unfaithful to their husbands so long as they were not found out.

A great number of the elder Statesmen and distinguished noblemen like the Duke were very anxious that in the reign of the young Victoria, the licentiousness of the last two Monarchs should be forgotten.

Granted, William IV had with his wife, Adelaide, done their best to create a very different atmosphere at Buckingham Palace and at Windsor from that created by the raffishness of George IV with his fat and elderly mistresses.

But King William had ten illegitimate children by Mrs. Jordan, the actress, so it was difficult for many people to take his reforms very seriously.

Queen Victoria was a shining example to the nation because she was not only too young to be anything but pure and proper, but everyone knew that when she had been told that she was to be Queen, she had said determinedly:

"I will be good!"

Prince Albert was her exact counterpart. At eleven years of age he had recorded in his diary:

"I intend to train myself to be a good and useful man."

It was not surprising that Buckingham Palace took on a different flavour with two such exceptional young people, and the whole country geared itself to a Puritanism which was the swing of the pendulum away from the impropriety of Victoria's badly behaved uncles.

Sorilda had been brought up to believe, because her mother had told her so, that women should be a good influence not only in their contact with everyone they met, but particularly they should guide and inspire their husbands and their children.

Reading her books of history, Sir Walter Scott's novels where good always triumphed over evil, and Jane Austen, where ladies and gentlemen lived exemplary lives, Sorilda had believed that she would marry when she found a man whom she loved and who loved her.

She was not important enough, she thought, even though she was the niece of a Duke, to have an arranged marriage, as happened in the Royal Houses and between the great aristocratic families in every country.

Sometimes she imagined the man who would be her husband, and always he was clever and charming and very much in love, as her father had been.

It was only when the new Duchess tried in every way to make her unattractive, and to keep her from meeting even the old men like her Uncle's friends who came to the Castle, that she began to visualise a long life of spinsterhood.

She would, she thought, be eternally a drudge to the demanding woman who hated her and there would be no possibility of changing her circumstances.

Had her Step-aunt been the same age as her Uncle, there would have been the chance that she might die, but Iris was only twenty-five, seven years older than herself, Sorilda thought, and certainly tough enough to survive her.

"What am I to do, Mama?" she had often asked in the darkness of the night.

In the coldness of her bedroom, hearing the wind whistling round the battlements in the Norman Towers, she felt that there was no-one to answer because even her mother had forsaken her.

Now suddenly, unexpectedly, the door of her prison was open and she could leave, not in the way she would have chosen, but at the same time it was an escape.

Sorilda tried to pray but no words would come.

Instead she was conscious only of an apprehension that was so acute that it was actually an inexpressible fear, and the uncomfortable knowledge that tomorrow she would have to face her Step-aunt.

'She will not wish me to marry the Earl,' she thought, and knew with just a flicker of satisfaction that there would be nothing Iris could do about it.

* * *

"There is no need for you to have a wedding-gown," the Duchess said, and her voice, as it had been ever since they had met that morning, was like a whiplash.

Sorilda had no way of knowing what had happened between husband and wife after the Duke and her Step-aunt had retired to bed.

But there was no doubt that the Duchess's beauty was overshadowed when she appeared downstairs just before noon.

There were dark lines under her eyes and Sorilda suspected, although she had no way of ascertaining whether it was the truth, that the Duke had slept alone in his own bedroom.

At any rate, he was up early to go riding.

Sorilda had anticipated this and had therefore not gone to the stables as usual. Instead she stayed in bed until she was called, thinking that last night must have been a nightmare and could never have taken place.

She had, however, only to hear the manner in which the Duchess spoke to her to know that it was the truth, and her Step-aunt was in fact furious, as she had expected, that she was to marry the Earl.

"If I am not to have a wedding-gown, and there is obviously no time," Sorilda asked now, "what do you suggest I wear?"

"Anything will do! You cannot imagine that the Earl will look at you!"

The Duchess spoke spitefully, and then, as if afraid that she had been overheard, she looked over her shoulder at the door.

They were alone in the Drawing-Room and the Duke, having returned from his ride, was interviewing his Agent, having, Sorilda learnt, sent a groom to London first thing with a note of apology for not being present at the meeting to which he had been specially invited by the Queen.

"I cannot think why you could not have told your Uncle you had no wish to be married," the Duchess went on.

"Do you suppose he would have listened to me?"

"I have been thinking . . ." the Duchess continued as if she had not spoken, "you could tell him that your religious convictions prevent you from marrying anyone as worldly as the Earl."

There was a pause before she added:

"Or why do you not suggest that you are contemplating entering a Convent?"

"Because it would not be true."

Sorilda faced the Duchess and suddenly she found that she was no longer frightened of her.

Until this moment she had always felt herself cringe every time Iris spoke to her in the disparaging, bitter manner which caused her to feel insignificant and an encumbrance.

But now at this moment her fear had gone and she knew that it was because she could escape.

"I refuse," she said firmly, "completely and absolutely refuse to be married in one of those hideous fawn gowns you have made me wear ever since you married Uncle Edmund."

The Duchess was astonished.

"How dare you speak to me like that!" she said angrily. "You will go to your Uncle and say what I have told you to say. It might prevent this disastrous marriage from taking place."

"Even if I do not marry the Earl," Sorilda replied, "I think you will find it difficult to see him again."

The Duchess made a sound of sheer fury and, reaching out her hand, slapped Sorilda in the face.

She was not expecting it and staggered for a moment beneath the blow; then she said very quietly:

"If you do that again I shall go to Uncle Edmund and tell him the truth."

"He will not believe you."

"He was clever enough to realise why the Earl came to my room," Sorilda retorted, "and that it was I who warned you of his arrival."

The Duchess bit her lip for a moment; then, losing her temper completely, she stamped her foot.

"Marry him then, if you are so determined to get yourself a title! But make no mistake, he will make you the most unhappy woman there has ever been! And I shall be delighted—yes, delighted!"

She walked from the Drawing-Room at the last words, slamming the door behind her, and Sorilda, although her heart was beating furiously at her own courage, gave a little laugh.

Her cheek hurt from the force of the Duchess's slap. At the same time, she knew that she had won the battle, and after so many months of subjection that was a solace in itself.

At the same time, she told herself that she would not go to her wedding looking drab and hideous with her hair greased down and without a crinoline.

The wedding would take place tomorrow and there was no time to buy anything.

The small towns between the Castle and London, like Bedford and St. Albans, would not have anything fitting for her to wear, and the same applied to Northampton.

If they could have waited a little longer she might have been able to make herself something which would at least have been more becoming than the hideous fawn gowns or the dull grey ones that the Duchess had insisted on buying her.

For a moment Sorilda wondered if she should appeal to her Uncle to postpone the wedding, then told herself that not only was he unlikely to agree, but if she delayed, her Step-aunt would find some "just cause or impediment" why the marriage should not take place.

Sorilda knew that Iris was wildly jealous of her becoming the Earl's wife, and she suspected, although she could not be sure, that she was really in love with him.

It was, Sorilda thought, not her idea of love. There certainly could be nothing spiritual about it.

At the same time, whether from her regret at losing the Earl or from the manner in which the Duke was treating her, there was no doubt as the day passed that the Duchess was unhappy besides being afraid for her own security.

For the first time since she had married, she literally fawned on the Duke, gazing beseechingly with her beautiful pale blue eyes into his, and speaking to him wistfully like a child who has been punished unfairly.

The Duke was sarcastic and icily cold in a manner that Sorilda had never known before and it was obviously a shock to his wife.

Sorilda, however, refused to be deeply concerned with them and determined to concentrate on herself.

She went up to her bedroom and looked at the gowns hanging in her wardrobe and thought that each one was more revoltingly ugly than the last.

Then despairingly she climbed up to the attics where the trunks she had brought with her on her parents' death had been stored away.

She opened one which contained her father's clothes, and as she looked at them she felt the tears gathering in her eyes and realised that there had never been a moment since his death when she had not missed him and longed for him to be with her.

It was agony to know that they would never talk together again and she could not ask him questions so that his answers could stimulate her mind.

She shut the trunk and opened another, which had belonged to her mother.

When her mother died Sorilda had been only fifteen, and most of her mother's clothes had been given away to friends who were not well off, and they had not only been glad to have them for their own use but also as a souvenir of the lady they had loved.

'There will be nothing for me here,' Sorilda thought despondently.

Then she came across a whalebone foundation that her mother had acquired just before she died.

It had been very revolutionary at the time, as the crinoline had barely come into fashion, but her mother had always been up-to-date.

Sorilda remembered that she had bought it for a period of mourning when she had bemoaned the fact that she must wear black for a very distant cousin.

"Why should I drape myself in crêpe for Cousin Adelaide?" she had asked her husband. "Always a tiresome, querulous old woman, she went out of her way to be disagreeable to you, which I found hard to forgive."

"The British are addicted to mourning," her father had replied jokingly, "and luckily, my darling, it becomes you a great deal more than it does most women.

"In fact," he added as he put his arm round her mother, "with your red hair and white skin, black makes you most improperly seductive!"

Her mother had laughed, and now as Sorilda recalled the conversation, from under the whalebone foundation she drew out a gown that, although it was black, was exactly the sort of dress which she thought she should wear for her wedding, but in white.

The bodice was very tight with a soft chiffon which was fine enough to be transparent over the back.

It was not surprising, Sorilda thought, that her father had found her mother alluring because not only was her magnolia-white skin framed by the black gown, but it accentuated the red of her hair and the emerald-green of her eyes.

She could remember her mother's lovely mouth

curving into a smile as she had looked at herself in
the mirror before they had gone off to the family fu-
neral.

"Papa's staid Eaton relations will be horrified by
my appearance," she exclaimed, "but after all, what
can they say? I am wearing black with not a patch of
colour anywhere."

It was her mother who provided the colour, Sorilda thought, and she told herself that that was exactly
what she had omitted to provide in the last six months
when the Duchess had overshadowed her life.

The colour of laughter had not only curved her
mother's lips, it had glinted in her eyes and seemed
to sparkle in her hair.

Everything they had done together had been fun,
and there had been a kind of joyousness about their
home which Sorilda had never found at the Castle and
which she missed unbearably.

It had been created by love, the love of her parents for each other and for her, and it had made life
an enchantment and their difficulties an adventure.

Then suddenly, sitting at the side of the trunk
and holding her mother's black gown in her hands,
Sorilda felt ashamed of herself.

'Mama would not have given in so easily,' she
thought. 'She would have fought back in her own
inimitable way and would have beaten the Duchess as
I was unable to do.'

She remembered how her mother had made everybody who knew her happy. They had brought her
their troubles, she had listened to them, and somehow she had always found a solution.

She had made people see, however dark things
looked, that they had something to be thankful for,
and they had gone away from her counting their blessings instead of their miseries.

"How foolish I have been, Mama," Sorilda told
her mother.

Although she knew that it was because she had
been so young, had no experience, and was alone that

she had allowed herself to become so despondent, now she felt that she had betrayed her mother's memory.

"I will fight for what I want and for what is right," she vowed now. "I will start again, in a very different way, but you will have to help me, Mama. I cannot do it by myself."

She felt the tears running down her cheeks as she spoke, but they were not the tears she had shed so bitterly in the past months.

They were tears of resolution—tears that brought with them a new courage and a new hope for the future.

"Help me, help me, Mama," she begged again.

Then suddenly as she bent and pressed her lips against the black gown which had belonged to her mother, she knew what she would wear at her wedding.

Chapter Four

There was a knock on the door and Sorilda turned from the mirror in which she had been looking at her reflection.

"Who is it?"

"It's Harriet, Miss Sorilda. Her Grace told me to arrange your hair and help you into your dress."

"I can manage quite well on my own, thank you, Harriet."

"But Her Grace..." the maid began to expostulate.

Then her voice stopped and she was obviously returning to her mistress to report that Sorilda would not let her enter the bedroom.

Sorilda's lips curled in a little smile because she knew how angry her Step-aunt would be. Then she saw a look of apprehension in her green eyes reflected in the mirror, and she lifted her chin proudly.

She need not be afraid; she was leaving the Castle and her Step-aunt and there was no longer any reason for her to be frightened and subservient.

Again she looked at herself in the mirror and knew that her very appearance gave her a courage she had never had before.

Her mother's gown with its full skirt over the whalebone crinoline swung out from her tiny waist, and its blackness accentuated the magnolia whiteness of her skin and the red in her hair.

She had washed it this morning and she had no intention of letting Harriet ruin it with her horrible dark pomade or destroy the soft waves of the hair on either side of her face.

Sorilda would have been very stupid if she had not realised that she not only looked lovely but also completely different from her appearance ever since she had grown up.

The black gave her a sophistication as well as an elegance, and when she picked up her mother's bonnet to complete the whole ensemble, she knew that she might have stepped straight out of a fashion-page of a ladies' magazine.

The bonnet with its brim edged with soft lace, its crown encircled with chiffon to match the gown, had been the very latest vogue three years ago, and Sorilda thought that perhaps only a woman would think it slightly dated.

At the same time, she knew that any man, including her Uncle and her future husband, would be astounded at the thought of a bride wearing black.

"I have no alternative," she said to herself.

Then she thought that even if she had, it was a joy and in a way an inspiration to wear anything which had belonged to her mother.

She was conscious of the soft sweet fragrance of violets, which was the perfume her mother had always used and which impregnated everything she wore and the rooms in which she moved.

It was very unlike the heavy exotic scent that Iris used, which Sorilda had often thought was out-of-place in the country and especially in the Castle.

"Help me, Mama," she said aloud.

Even as she spoke the words very softly, someone tried the handle of the door.

Sorilda had locked it, and a moment later the Duchess's voice, sharp and imperious, cried:

"Open the door, Sorilda! I cannot imagine why you should wish to lock yourself in."

"I want to be alone."

"Alone?" the Duchess exclaimed.

She could not believe that anyone could ever have made such a request before and her voice rose as she said:

"I have never heard such nonsense! I want to speak to you and see if you are properly dressed."

"I want to be alone," Sorilda replied, "until it is time for me to go downstairs for my wedding."

She could imagine the fury on the Duchess's face because she was being defied. She thought too that she heard her stamp her foot before she said:

"I have never heard of anything so preposterous! Open the door immediately! That is an order!"

Sorilda glanced at the clock.

"In ten minutes," she said quietly, "I shall no longer have to take orders from you, and for that short time I wish to think about my future."

She knew that her reply made the Duchess gasp and for the moment she was bereft of words in which to answer.

And then, with a sound of exasperation and anger, she walked away.

Despite the fact that she had sounded so brave, Sorilda gave a little sigh of relief. It was hard, after being bullied for so many months, to realise that what she had said was the truth.

She would no longer have to take orders from the Duchess, but only from a man who had no wish to marry her and who, she was sure, was at this moment as apprehensive about the future as she was.

Then Sorilda forced herself to remember that the only thing that mattered was that the Earl was her means of escape.

She walked to the window and stood looking out at the Park. She remembered how she had thought herself a Royal prisoner incarcerated in an impregnable Castle.

But now the nightmare was over and the only thing to be feared was that she might be escaping from one prison only to enter another.

Instinctively she began to pray to her mother for help and to God, Whom she had thought at times in these last unhappy months had forsaken her.

But she knew now that she had not been forgotten, she had not been lost, but was under His protection and He would always be there whatever the future might hold.

Deep in her thoughts and her prayers, Sorilda jumped when there came another knock on the door.

"Who is it?"

"His Grace has asked me to inform you, Miss Sorilda, that His Lordship is here."

Sorilda drew in her breath.

"Tell His Grace I will come down immediately."

"Very good, Miss."

Sorilda turned from the window and looked round the bedroom. Everything was in readiness.

She had unpacked her trunk, after the maids had packed it, and had thrown out all the hideous beige and grey gowns which her Step-aunt had chosen for her. She had also discarded most of the nightgowns and underclothes that she had worn before she had considered herself grown-up.

In her mother's trunk upstairs she had found delicate, fine lawn nightgowns trimmed with lace, silk petticoats that rustled when she walked, and a number of other garments, all so exquisite that Sorilda had gasped with delight. She had really forgotten that they were there and she had not examined before what remained of her mother's possessions, for the simple reason that she had thought that to do so would make her cry.

It had never crossed her mind that she might wear her mother's clothes, but now she knew that everything she put on that had belonged to her mother would strengthen the courage which was already coursing through her veins.

Practically everything in her trunk now had been her mother's, including a black evening-gown as beautiful and attractive as the dress she was wearing for her wedding.

"The first thing I will do," Sorilda vowed to herself, "is buy new clothes of my own choice."

She bundled everything that had been chosen for her by her Step-aunt into the bottom of her wardrobe, shut the door, and turned the key. Then she strapped up her trunk, knowing that she had with her the only things she wished to wear.

Lying on the chair was the silk shawl with long fringe which her mother had bought to go with the gown. There were also a pair of expensive black suede gloves and a little bag in the same silk material as the bodice.

In another trunk Sorilda had packed no garments but all the small objects that she treasured and which had belonged to her mother: her work-box; a miniature of her father and one of herself when she was a child; books bound in leather which her mother had loved and packed very carefully in masses of protective paper; and the ornaments that had stood on the mantelshelf in her bedroom and by her bed.

"Wherever I am," Sorilda told herself, "they will make me feel at home because they belonged to Mama."

Slowly and without haste she put on the long suede gloves; then, picking up her shawl and her bag, she unlocked the door and started to walk along the corridor towards the stairs.

Nervous though she was, she could not help a little feminine thrill because of the swing of her crinoline and the knowledge that, strange though her gown might appear for a bride, she could for the first time face her Step-aunt on equal terms as an attractive woman.

When she reached the top of the stairs, Sorilda saw that her Uncle was waiting below in the Hall, and he was alone.

She knew when she saw him that the Earl and her

Step-aunt would have gone ahead to the Chapel, and she thought scornfully that the Duchess would have seized the opportunity of being able to talk to the Earl if only for a few seconds.

"They are both despicable and I hate them!" Sorilda told herself, and lifted her head even higher as she walked slowly down the stairs.

When she reached the Hall she realised that her Uncle was staring at her in amazement.

She moved across the marble floor towards him and when she reached his side he exclaimed:

"Black! Whatever possessed you to wear black for your wedding?"

"I should have thought it was quite appropriate, Uncle Edmund," Sorilda replied. "But actually it is the only gown I possess that does not make me feel as if I have stepped out of an Orphanage!"

The Duke looked at her in perplexity and she explained:

"I have not been allowed to choose my own gowns lately, but this is my own choice, to which I think I am fully entitled!"

"At any rate it is too late to change," the Duke said.

He offered her his arm as he spoke, and they walked down the long corridor which led to the Chapel.

Afterwards Sorilda could never quite remember the Service or exactly what she said or did.

She was in fact vividly conscious from the moment she stood beside the Earl that waves of anger were emanating from him in a manner that she would have found terrifying if she had not had some small sympathy for him.

"After all," she told herself, "however badly he has behaved, it was at my Step-aunt's invitation that he came to the Castle."

He was unmarried and therefore could seek his amusement where he wished.

It might be reprehensible and a sin to pursue his neighbour's wife, but Sorilda could not help feeling that the real guilt must rest on Iris's white shoulders.

She did not fail to notice when the ceremony was over and they walked from the Chapel towards the Hall that the Duchess had taken pains to make herself look even more alluring than usual.

Her blue gown, exactly the shade of her eyes, would have been spectacular at Buckingham Palace, and the diamonds round her neck and in her ears made her sparkle like a Christmas-tree.

As she looked at her Step-aunt, Sorilda saw an expression in her eyes which told her that whoever he might have married, Iris still desired the man who had climbed up the steps of the West Tower to her bed-room.

'Uncle Edmund has certainly made the punish-ment fit the crime,' Sorilda thought, and wondered if the Earl would visit his fury upon her once they were alone.

There were no warm farewells to the newly mar-ried couple. The Duke did not shake hands with the Earl nor did he kiss his niece.

He merely watched grimly as a footman placed Sorilda's shawl round her shoulders, the Butler handed the Earl his hat and gloves, and they walked down the steps to where Sorilda saw a Phaeton waiting.

She thought with a little sigh of relief that at least they would not be cooped up together in the intimacy of a carriage.

She was helped into the Phaeton by a flunkey, the Earl picked up the reins, a groom ran from the horses' heads to climb up onto the seat behind them, and they were off.

It was curiosity which made Sorilda glance back to see that her Uncle and Step-aunt had not waited to watch them depart. There was no-one at the top of the steps except the Major Domo and a number of footmen.

They drove up the drive and after a little while Sorilda felt the tenseness which had been with her ever since she had entered the Chapel relax a little.

She was married!

She still could not believe that it had really happened, that she was driving away from the Castle and no longer could her Step-aunt rage at her!

No longer would she have to submit to the humiliation and misery that had made her feel that every day was darker and more menacing than the last.

Almost as if in response to her feelings, the sun came out from behind a cloud to shine golden through the branches of the trees and glisten on the silver harness of the four magnificent horses the Earl was driving.

They passed through the lodge-gates and now as they reached the centre of the small village the Earl, instead of continuing left towards Winsford Park, turned right.

Sorilda turned her head and looked at him questioningly.

"We are going to London," he said.

He spoke uncompromisingly and even beneath those few brief words Sorilda could hear his anger.

She did not reply but she thought she understood. He could not at the moment face the surprise and speculation of his own household if he should suddenly return, within an hour of leaving, accompanied by a wife.

She felt that at his London home everything would be less personal and his staff would not expect so many explanations.

He drove on until when it was nearly two o'clock and Sorilda was just beginning to feel that she was decidedly hungry, the Earl drove his horses into the courtyard of a Coaching-Inn.

There were a number of vehicles in the yard, Phaetons and carriages, and Sorilda felt a sense of relief that there would be a number of other people in the Dining-Room and they would not have the discomfort of being alone.

However, after she had washed and tidied her hair, which had been a little blown owing to the speed at which they had travelled, she came down the ancient oak stairs to find a servant waiting to lead her to a private room.

The Earl was there and she found herself thinking not only how elegant he was but also that his handsome face made her in some small degree understand her Step-aunt's passion for him.

"Will you have a glass of Madeira?"

She knew as the Earl spoke that he forced the words to his lips, and she thought too that he deliberately did not look at her, as if he could not bear the sight of the woman he had married.

"Thank you," Sorilda replied. "But only a little. I do not like Madeira very much."

"Then of course you must have anything you like," the Earl said. "I suppose champagne would be appropriate for the occasion."

His tone was sarcastic but Sorilda replied quite pleasantly:

"I think that would be very nice. Papa always said when he was driving long distances he preferred champagne to anything else."

The Earl pulled the bell with a violence which made Sorilda think it was surprising that it did not come away in his hand.

When the servant appeared and the Earl had given the order for the champagne, Sorilda thought he was about to say something to her, but before he could do so, the Landlord followed by two mob-capped maids came into the room, carrying their luncheon.

The choice was quite considerable and the food, although plain, was well cooked.

It was impossible to say anything intimate while they were being waited on, and Sorilda was glad that she would have a chance to eat before she had to encounter what she was certain would be a difficult moment.

She had found it impossible to eat anything at

breakfast-time and had merely drunk a cup of coffee, and now because she was alone with the man she had married she felt as if there were a hundred butterflies fluttering about in her breasts.

She managed, however, to eat quite a sensible amount before she began to feel once again that the food would choke her.

However, the champagne helped, and she hoped, although she could not dare to say so, that it was helping the Earl as well.

He certainly drank a large amount of the bottle, and then without exchanging more than half-a-dozen words they were on their way again.

Now Sorilda realised that the Earl was pushing his horses as if he wished to reach their destination as quickly as was humanly possible.

It was, however, quite a long time before they reached the outskirts of London, and finally, with the horses sweating from the speed at which they had travelled, they drew up outside Winsford House in Park Lane.

It was certainly very impressive, Sorilda thought, but she had no time to take in anything before she was helped down from the Phaeton and moved ahead of the Earl into a large Hall.

"I hope Your Lordship has had a good journey?" an elderly Butler asked.

"You received my instructions?" the Earl enquired sharply.

"The groom arrived two hours ago, M'Lord. Everything has been seen to."

The Earl walked to Sorilda's side.

"My Housekeeper—Mrs. Dawson—will show you to your room," he said abruptly. "I expect you would like to rest. We dine at eight o'clock."

He bowed perfunctorily, still, Sorilda noticed, without looking directly at her, and walked away before she could reply.

For a moment she stared after him, feeling unsure of herself, and then the Butler said gravely:

"Will you follow me, M'Lady."

From the way he addressed her Sorilda knew that the Earl had, in his communication to his London household, informed them of his marriage.

She followed the Butler upstairs and on the landing found the Housekeeper, rustling in black silk, waiting for her.

She was a middle-aged woman with a kind face, and, having curtseyed, she led Sorilda along the passage and opened a door into a large, magnificently furnished bedroom.

"Would you like to rest in bed, M'Lady," the Housekeeper asked, "or on the chaise-longue?"

"As it is some time before I need dress for dinner," Sorilda answered, "I think I would rather go to bed."

"The maids'll unpack your luggage in the dressing-room, Your Ladyship, as soon as it is brought upstairs."

"Thank you," Sorilda said with a smile.

It was as if her smile broke through the Housekeeper's self-control and her feelings.

"Oh! M'Lady!" she exclaimed. "I know His Lordship has wished for no words of congratulation, but I have to tell you how pleased we all are to hear of his marriage and to someone as lovely as Your Ladyship."

"Thank you," Sorilda replied.

"We have been hoping for ever so long, for years in fact, that His Lordship would take a wife, and when the groom arrived with the news, you could have knocked me down with a feather!"

"It must have been a surprise," Sorilda murmured.

"It was indeed! But a very pleasant one. I do wish Your Ladyship every happiness."

"Thank you," Sorilda replied, but she thought that with the Earl's attitude, that was very unlikely.

But she told herself that nothing mattered except that she was free of the Castle and her Step-aunt!

When she had undressed and put on one of her

mother's lovely nightgowns, she lay in the huge comfortable bed, thinking that at least the Earl's household were not aware of the reason for his precipitate marriage.

She had a feeling, however, that in the country it would be difficult for them not to guess that there was some ulterior motive for such a sudden change in his life.

The grooms would have known that he had taken a horse out the night before last, and someone at Winsford Park would have received the note that the Duchess had written and Jim had carried from the Castle to the Earl.

'They will put two and two together,' Sorilda thought.

She could understand that the Earl could not bear to face the staff who had served him and doubtless his father before him for so many years.

She must have been tired, for she slept for a little while and awoke when a maid came to tell her that her bath was ready.

She knew when she dressed herself in the other black gown which had belonged to her mother that the maid and the Housekeeper were surprised that she should wear anything so sombre on her wedding-night. But she had no intention of giving them an explanation and hoped that they would imagine that she was in deep mourning.

Only as she was ready to go downstairs did she say:

"Tomorrow I wish to go shopping, and as I am quite certain it is something which would not interest His Lordship, perhaps you, Mrs. Dawson, will accompany me."

"I shall be very pleased to do so, M'Lady," the Housekeeper replied, obviously gratified by the invitation.

She paused before she added a little tentatively, as if she was afraid of being impertinent:

"Your Ladyship is very beautiful and black is un-doubtedly extremely becoming. At the same time, as a bride I'd wish to see Your Ladyship in white."

"I will buy a white gown tomorrow," Sorilda promised. "Good-night, and thank you for looking after me."

"Elsie will be sitting up, M'Lady, so please ring the bell when you come upstairs. Unless you prefer her to wait here in the bedroom?"

"No, I will ring," Sorilda answered.

"Thank you, M'Lady."

Mrs. Dawson opened the door and curtseyed.

Sorilda walked into the passage and as she moved towards the stairs she could see herself reflected in several mirrors which graced the walls. She might almost have been her mother passing by, and she was un-ashamedly delighted with her own appearance.

The low-cut dress was draped softly round her bare shoulders, and in the Drawing-Room the candles and the chandeliers were already lit and Sorilda knew that they would not only glitter on her hair but on the diamond necklace she wore round her neck.

It had belonged to her mother, and her jewel-box containing it and other items of jewellery had been brought to her bedroom earlier in the morning by one of the maids.

"His Grace's compliments, Miss. He thought you would wish to take these with you."

Sorilda had almost forgotten that she owned them.

The jewels had been taken away from her as soon as she had arrived at the Castle and she had never thought to ask for them.

When she had opened the leather jewel-case she had found inside in the velvet-lined compartments the diamond necklace, bracelets, rings, ear-rings to match, and also two diamond stars that her mother had often worn in her hair.

There was nothing of very great value, but at the

same time when she looked at them Sorilda felt her eyes moist with tears because they meant so much to her.

Tonight, when she had fastened her mother's necklace round her neck she had felt it was almost a breast-plate in which she could go out and defy the enemy who was her husband.

She could feel her silk petticoats rustle as she moved over the carpet to where he was standing at the far end of the Drawing-Room against a carved marble mantelpiece.

If he had looked smart and elegant in his day-clothes, in evening-dress he was, Sorilda thought, so magnificent that she felt herself staring at him in a be-mused fashion like a village yokel.

Then the frowning anger of his expression made her forget everything but a feeling of shyness because they were alone.

"A glass of champagne?" the Earl asked. "I thought that was what you would expect."

As he spoke, Sorilda realised that a servant had entered the room behind her, carrying champagne on a tray. She took a glass from it and raised it to her lips.

The Earl had drawn his watch from his waistcoat pocket and was comparing it with the clock on the mantelpiece.

"Unless I am wrong," he said aloud, "dinner is late."

At that moment the Butler announced at the door:
"Dinner is served, M'Lady."

Sorilda waited for the Earl to offer her his arm but he did not do so, and as he started to walk towards the door, she moved beside him.

The Dining-Room was as impressive as the rest of the house. There were a number of portraits round the walls, besides a display of gold ornaments which she was sure had been in the family for generations.

There was also a decoration of white flowers on the table. Sorilda saw the Earl glance at it and she knew that it was something which he had not ordered but which had been done by the servants as the correct procedure for their wedding-dinner.

If Sorilda had not been so nervous she would have laughed at the manner in which the Earl, on sitting down at the head of the table, deliberately and disdainfully flicked aside some white roses which seemed to encroach upon his plate.

Because Sorilda thought that with a Butler and four footmen waiting on them it would look ridiculous for them to sit in stony silence, she said:

"I am sure you must have broken a record today by the speed in which we reached London. It has always taken me much longer in the past."

For a second the Earl looked as if he was surprised that she had a voice and could use it. Then he replied:

"It usually takes me two-and-a-half hours from here to the country. Today, I agree, we must have done it quicker."

"Your horses are very fine."

"I like to think so."

There was silence. He was making it very difficult, Sorilda thought. However much he disliked her, they should surely act their parts with dignity in front of the servants.

The food was delicious although Sorilda thought there were too many courses, until it struck her that the staff were trying their best to celebrate a marriage in which the bridegroom, at any rate, was making the worst of the situation!

"Have you any plans for tomorrow morning?" Sorilda asked.

"Tomorrow morning?" the Earl repeated.

"I would like to go shopping."

"Yes, yes, of course. A carriage will be at your disposal."

"Thank you."

Again there was silence and Sorilda began to feel cross. After all, he might at least try to keep up appearances and, even if he was angry, to be polite.

She guessed that because he was so good-looking he was very spoilt. Women like her Step-aunt would find him irresistible, and he would have done whatever he liked, not only with them but in every other way ever since he had inherited the title.

She remembered how Huxley had related with envy the list of Classical races he had won.

This would go to a sportsman's head and perhaps this was the first time in his life that the Earl had been manoeuvred into a disadvantageous position from which he could not extricate himself.

Dinner at last came to an end, the servants withdrew from the room, and Sorilda said:

"Do you wish me to leave you to your port, or rather the brandy which I see you are drinking?"

For the moment the Earl did not reply and then he said:

"I suppose we should have a talk."

"It would certainly be better than sitting in an uncomfortable silence!"

She did not mean to be aggressive, but his failure to respond to her efforts had annoyed her.

The Earl raised his eye-brows in surprise. Then he said:

"I find it difficult to discourse in an easy manner with a complete stranger."

"That I can understand," Sorilda answered; "at the same time, if we are to be rude to each other, I think it is a mistake to do so in front of the servants."

If she had fired a shot into the air the Earl could not have been more astonished. Then he said:

"I imagine you are questioning my good manners, and you may be right, but you can hardly expect me to accept this situation with equanimity."

"You seem to forget, My Lord, that I am in the same position as you are!" Sorilda replied. "Perhaps I should express my regret that I interfered instead of allowing my Uncle to come into the house without your being aware of it."

The Earl glanced at her, then rose to his feet and said:

"We will go where we are not likely to be over-heard."

As he spoke, he refilled his glass with brandy and walked across the room to open the door for Sorilda.

She passed him without speaking but was aware as she walked down the passage ahead of him that her heart was thumping heavily in her breast.

'The battle has begun,' she thought, 'and I won-der what will be the end of it and who will win.'

She walked into the Drawing-Room, thinking with one part of her mind how attractive the room was, while another part was conscious that it was difficult to breathe and she had the uncomfortable suspicion that her hands were trembling.

She sat down on a chair at the side of the fire-place, aware, as she did so, that her dress billowed out in a very attractive manner and that scent of her mother's violets soothed her agitation.

"Help me, Mama," she prayed silently, "help me!"

Then she waited for the Earl to speak.

He stood in front of the fireplace, his chin stuck out a little, his eyes dark.

"This whole situation is intolerable," he began sharply. "If you had said you did not wish to marry me, your Uncle would not have forced you to do so."

Now Sorilda realised why he was so angry with her. He thought that in some way she could have prevented the ceremony from taking place.

She thought for a moment before she answered quietly:

"He might have listened to me, although I very much doubt it. However, as it happened, I wished to be your wife."

The Earl looked at her incredulously.

"You wished to be my wife?" he repeated slowly. "Having never met me, knowing that I was interested in your Step-aunt? Do you expect me to accept that as the truth?"

"It is, as it happens, completely true," Sorilda said slowly, "not, may I add quickly, because I was enamoured with you personally, but because you were a way of escape from what had become for me an intolerable situation."

"I do not understand."

"It is quite simple. The Duchess loathes me and has made my life a complete hell."

"That I find hard to believe!" the Earl interposed.

"Whether you believe me or not, it is a fact," Sorilda said. "And as I was never allowed to met anyone, least of all a man, I thought I would be forced to live at the Castle until I died."

There was a note of sincerity in her voice which was unmistakable, and the Earl stared at her until he gave a sudden laugh which had no humour in it.

"So that was why you were so willing to help me."

"That was not my motive in the first place," Sorilda answered. "I warned you when Uncle Edmund arrived because I was thinking only of him. He had been kind to me in his own fashion and I did not want him to be desperately hurt, as he would have been—and in fact has been—by learning the truth."

"How do you know that?" the Earl enquired.

"He is intelligent enough to realise that you would not be visiting me in such a manner, nor would I have invited you to do so!"

Sorilda could not helping adding the last few words.

She saw the Earl's face darken before he said:

"I suppose recriminations will not help under the circumstances. What we have to discuss is our future."

Sorilda did not answer, she only sat looking at him, her eyes on his face.

"I have been thinking it over," he went on. "There appear to me to be only two alternatives."

"What are . . . they?"

"One, that we should live separate lives. I own a number of houses in different parts of the country and am quite prepared to put one entirely at your disposal."

He ceased speaking and after a moment Sorilda said in a rather small voice:

"What . . . is . . . the . . . other . . . alternative?"

As he spoke, it had suddenly struck her how frightening it would be to be entirely alone.

Even if she lived in one of the Earl's houses and had the Earl's money to spend, she could not at the moment visualise a life by herself with no-one to help and companion her.

"The other alternative," the Earl went on, "is to make the best of a bad job. I have always been told that sooner or later I would have to settle down and have an heir. I like being a bachelor and I would prefer to remain one, but that is now impossible."

Again there was silence, and then Sorilda said hesitatingly:

"I—I . . . understand . . . what you . . . are . . . suggesting . . . but . . . knowing what you felt . . . for . . . my . . . Step-aunt, you could . . . not . . . expect . . . me . . ."

"No, no, of course not! I did not mean that! We should try to get to know each other and at least have a trial period before we take steps to be more—intimate."

"That is what I should like," Sorilda replied quickly, "and I think that anything else might cause a scandal and a great deal of gossip which would harm you."

Again the Earl raised his eye-brows, and Sorilda explained:

"You have just received the Order of the Garter."

"I understand, and I suppose I should be grateful to you."

He spoke grudgingly and Sorilda gave a little smile.

"I have just been explaining why I am grateful to you. I would rather be here, however difficult you . . ."

She stopped, feeling that what she had been about to say was rude, and he interposed quickly:

"All right, I am difficult, and I do not pretend that this morning it was not a devilish effort to get myself to the Castle."

"I can . . . understand," Sorilda said, "but perhaps things may not be as . . . bad as you . . . expect, if we use a little . . . common sense."

The Earl gave a laugh and it was different from the one before.

"So that is what you call it," he said. "Personally, I can think of other, more apt descriptions, but never mind. May I ask you something?"

"But of course."

"What in the name of Heaven made you wear a black wedding-gown?"

"It is easy to answer that," Sorilda replied. "I had literally nothing else except some hideous garments chosen by my Step-aunt for the purpose of making me look as ugly as possible."

It seemed to her as she spoke that the Earl looked at her for the first time. His eyes seemed to take in the red of her hair, the white of her skin, and the glint in the green eyes raised to his.

His glance seemed very comprehensive before he said:

"I imagine she was jealous. I suppose I am lucky, since you might have been as plain as a pikestaff."

"That did cross my mind!" Sorilda replied.

He smiled.

"I will try to be a little more civilised than I have been today and say that it will be interesting to get to know you."

"May I reciprocate," Sorilda replied, "by telling you that there are a great many things I would like to know about your possessions, particularly your horses."

"You are interested in horses?"

"I watched you three days ago riding one horse which was particularly magnificent on the Long Gallop."

"You watched me!"

"I heard that you had bought two very fine animals at Tattersall's."

"How could you have heard?" the Earl began, then added: "That is a stupid question; there is nothing that goes on in my stables which is not immediately known in every other stable in the County!"

"And if they are interested in your horses you can understand that there are a number of people who are . . . interested in . . . you too."

"Were you?"

The question surprised her and she answered truthfully:

"Not as a man, but as the winner of the Gold Cup at Ascot and the Oaks."

The Earl put back his head and laughed, and this time it was a sound of genuine amusement.

"That is the truth straight from the shoulder," he said, "and I know of no other woman who would have been so frank."

"I am sorry if it . . . was . . . rude."

"No, no, not in the least," he said quickly. "I think that if we are going to build a marriage on any sort of sound foundation, frankness is essential."

"I agree. At the same time, you may not always . . . like what I say or . . . do!"

"Then I will be frank and tell you so."

"That will make everything . . . easier, and brings me to another . . . question."

"What is that?"

"How much . . . money can I . . . spend?"

The Earl looked at her in surprise and she explained:

"At the moment I have two gowns which belonged to my mother, the one you saw at our wedding and the other I am wearing now. I imagine for your wife that would be a somewhat restricted wardrobe!"

"Of course," the Earl said. "Spend what you like, and I have a feeling you will not bankrupt me."

"I believe I have a little money of my . . . own," Sorilda began.

"Forget it!" the Earl said. "Your Uncle did say something about it this morning, but I told him to communicate with my Solicitors. It is not of any importance, unless you wish to be independent."

"Not as far as money is concerned," Sorilda replied, "but I know I have not enough for what I wish to . . . spend."

Again the Earl laughed.

"You are beginning to frighten me."

"I have no wish to do that, but I hope I will . . . embellish my position as the . . . Countess of Winsford."

The Earl looked at her and then said slowly:

"I am quite certain that you will, but at the same time I am not sure that it will always be to my advantage."

Chapter Five

Sorilda was just about to reply when suddenly the door seemed to burst open.

As the Butler announced in a somewhat shaken voice: "Lady Alison Fane, M'Lord!" a woman passed him, rushing into the room in a manner which made Sorilda stare at her incredulously.

She ran towards the Earl, who had risen to his feet, and as she did so, Sorilda saw that she was extremely attractive with fair hair, not so gold as the Duchess's but still unmistakably fair, and with wide blue eyes that at the moment seemed to be dark with anger.

"Sholto!" she cried before she reached the Earl's side. "It is not true! Say it is not true!"

Her voice seemed to ring out so shrilly that Sorilda expected the crystal chandeliers to tinkle with the force of it. Then as the Earl did not seem to find words with which to reply, Lady Alison turned her head to look at Sorilda.

"Is this she? Could you possibly have been so treacherous, so cruel, so underhanded?"

Now she no longer shrieked and there was an unmistakable sob behind the words.

At last the Earl found his voice.

"I regret to find you so upset, Alison," he said.

"I had in fact intended to call upon you tomorrow morning."

"To tell me you were married?" Lady Alison asked, and now again she was furious. "When a few minutes ago at Lady Shrewsbury's Ball I was informed what had happened, I did not believe it!"

"How did Lady Shrewsbury know?" the Earl asked curiously.

"Apparently one of your servants told her Butler," Lady Alison replied, "but I should have thought, had you any sensibility, that I would have been the first to be informed of your intention to marry!"

Sorilda knew that the Earl was finding it difficult to explain. Before he could do so, Lady Alison went on:

"After all we have meant to each other, after all the love I have given you, the happiness we have found with each other, how could this happen, how could it? If you had decided to marry, why not marry me?"

"It is not exactly like that, Alison," the Earl began tentatively, but Lady Alison had not finished speaking.

Once again she was looking at Sorilda.

"What can this woman give you that I have not given you? By what means has she tricked you into marriage when you have always sworn that you would remain a bachelor?"

She gave a sudden shriek and flung up her hands dramatically.

"How could you have done this to me? How could you make me suffer in such a way? I love you, Sholto. Yes, I love you with my whole heart, and now I shall not only suffer the agonies of being forsaken, but also be a laughing-stock to all my friends!"

Lady Alison almost spat the words at him as she walked from the Earl to stand over Sorilda.

"I loathe you," she said, "and if I can hurt or injure you in any way, you may be quite certain I will do so! If you think you can keep the most elusive man in London in your clutches, you are very much mistaken. He will betray you as he has betrayed every other woman who has been foolish enough to lay her heart at his feet!"

She spoke so violently that for one moment Sorilda thought she was going to hit her, and she drew back apprehensively.

As if the Earl thought the same thing, he put a restraining hand on Lady Alison's arm, saying:

"I am sorry you should have heard of my marriage without warning, Alison. Tomorrow I will call on you and we will talk of what has happened."

"And will your new wife permit you to associate with your old loves?" Lady Alison asked spitefully. "Perhaps you have already explained that you flit from flower to flower, taking everything a woman can give and leaving her broken-hearted as undoubtedly you will leave your wife!"

"That is quite enough," the Earl said sternly. "Let me take you to your carriage, as I am sure you wish to go home now."

"You can hardly expect me to return to the Ball," Lady Alison said bitterly, "with everyone laughing at me, realising that I have joined the long queue of your discarded loves!"

Now once again her voice broke on the words. She turned from the Earl to walk towards the door.

He hurried after her and Sorilda could hear their voices in the Hall.

Several minutes passed before she could force herself to rise to her feet, feeling shaken and upset by what had occurred.

She had never before seen a woman lose her self-control as completely as Lady Alison had done, or speak with a wildness and anger which made her seem somehow common and vulgar like a woman of the streets.

She realised that her heart was beating uncomfortably fast and she told herself that if this was the sort of situation she would have to face in the future, she had no idea how she would cope with it.

Then as she drew a deep breath she told herself that it was the Earl's fault.

How could he pursue and make love to so many women? Lady Alison, her Step-aunt, and perhaps a great number more, making them so infatuated with him that they could behave in a manner which was reprehensible and degrading.

'If that is love,' Sorilda thought, 'I can only pray that I shall never experience it.'

Then she remembered how much her mother had loved her father and how very different it had been. The happiness and radiance between them was so close that they seemed almost to share the same thoughts.

She puzzled over the difference and came to the conclusion that what her Step-aunt and this other woman felt for the Earl was a love that had nothing spiritual about it. It was just a physical desire for possession.

Sorilda was very innocent; she did not understand what happened when the Earl made love to a woman such as her Step-aunt and they went to bed together.

All she knew was that even to think about it made her shrink inside as if from something unclean and unpleasant.

In that moment she knew that she would never be the Earl's wife in anything but name.

"If he wants to be more intimate with me," she told herself, "when he wishes me to give him the heir of which he spoke, then I shall go away!"

She had no idea when or how she would contrive it, but meanwhile she had the chance of living here in the Earl's house until she could see a little more clearly what lay ahead.

She thought that Lady Alison must by now have left and she could retire to bed before the Earl returned, but even as she decided to do so, he came in through the door, shutting it behind him.

"I can only apologise, Sorilda," he said, "for that very unnecessary and over-dramatic scene. Lady Alison forced her way into the house, or it would not have happened."

Sorilda looked at him coldly.

"I presume she would still have suffered whether she had seen you or not."

"Are you feeling sorry for her?" the Earl questioned.

There was something in the way he asked the question, the supercilious tone of his voice and the expression in his eyes, which made Sorilda feel angry.

"Without creating any more dramatics," she said in an icy voice, "I can only say with all sincerity that I am extremely sorry for any woman with whom you are associated!"

Without waiting for his reply, she walked away from him and, opening the door, let herself out into the Hall.

Then, frightened that he might follow her, she hurried up the stairs to her own room.

When she reached it she locked the door into the corridor and another which she suspected communicated with the Earl's bedroom.

Then she sat down on the chair to wait for the tumultuous beat of her heart to subside before she rang for a maid.

*   *   *

Sorilda came into the Hall followed by two footmen carrying a number of dress-boxes. She had now been in London for over a week and had spent every moment of the time shopping.

She had never before known the joy of buying exquisitely elegant gowns which gave her a new confidence as well as being a frame for a beauty that she had not realised she possessed.

The compliments of the dress-makers and later of the Earl's friends whom she met every night were an excitement that acted like champagne.

As if the Earl had no desire to be alone with her, he invited a succession of guests to dinner, many of whom came, Sorilda knew, out of curiosity to see what she was like.

She had luncheon alone, learning from the Secretary, Mr. Barnham, who came to see her every morning, that His Lordship was either engaged with Prince Albert or in attendance at the House of Lords.

If Sorilda had not been so busy disliking the Earl, she would have been fascinated to learn how many Committees he was on, a number of which concerned projects close to her heart.

But it was difficult, because she felt so incensed with him, not to feel a kind of tightening within her breasts when his name was mentioned, and there was an icy coldness in her voice when she spoke to him, although she was studiously polite as she realised he was trying to be.

At the same time, when she saw him at the head of the Dining-Room table with an attractive woman on either side of him, she could not help appreciating how handsome he was and how it was hard to find any other man in the room to compare with his elegance or his air of consequence.

"One can admire a horse," Sorilda told herself, "and still find him a difficult, unpredictable animal!"

The Earl undoubtedly had both those characteristics, and the conversations she overheard between his most staid and respectable friends left her in no doubt that the whole of London Society was astonished by the fact that he should have married anyone, least of all a woman who was unknown to them and who was so young.

Piecing together bits of information until like a puzzle they made a complete picture, Sorilda realised that the Earl's love-affairs had always been conducted with women who were married, like her Step-aunt, or widowed, like Lady Alison.

She could not help telling herself scornfully that he was in fact a Casanova in his conquests, and the women whom he had induced to love him would soon be too numerous for him to count!

She would hear snatches of conversation when she entered a room, or moved from one group to another, which told her a great deal about her husband.

"Charlotte is broken-hearted . . ."

"Adelaide was certain that he would marry no-one and is extremely piqued . . ."

"Georgina says she will not entertain the new Countess whatever anyone may . . ."

As those who spoke realised that Sorilda was listening, their voices would break off in mid-air.

But she had heard enough and her lips would curl disdainfully and she could look at the Earl with what she hoped he would recognise as contempt in her eyes.

After the first night he behaved in a polished and exemplary manner, so she actually had no complaints and there were no more scenes such as Lady Alison had made.

But Sorilda was aware that at every Ball or Reception they attended there were lovely woman who looked at her balefully and who would, she was quite certain, had they obeyed their impulses, have stuck a dagger into her!

She had the satisfaction of realising, after the first two or three Balls, that she was more of a success than she had dared to hope.

She knew that her new gowns had a great deal to do with it and also the fact that Mr. Barnham had told her that on the Earl's instructions, the Winsford family jewels were at her disposal.

Never had Sorilda imagined that except in some mythical Aladdin's Cave could there be such a magnificent selection of gems from which she could choose.

There were sets of almost every conceivable precious stone, ranging from tiaras down to buckles for the shoes, and there were also ropes of pearls of every size as well as jewelled vanity-cases, jewelled handles for sun-shades, and jewelled clasps to be attached to handbags to match the gown she was wearing.

She began to feel as if she were a child who had been let loose in a sweet-shop, and she would visit Mr. Barnham's office where the safe was kept and discuss with him which tiara would complement her gown and which jewels she would wear to dazzle the dinner-party or the Ball to which they were proceeding that evening.

It was such an unbelievable change from the drab misery of the Castle that sometimes she was afraid she would wake up and find herself dressed in one of her hideous fawn gowns and being nagged on by the Duchess to the verge of tears.

Now she was not in the least tearful but ready to fight the Earl if necessary to get everything she wanted.

In a way, it was slightly deflating to find that she never got the chance to exchange any words with him that were not overheard.

Sometimes, because she wished to talk to him alone, even if disagreeably, she would wait in the Dining-Room at the time she knew he had to return to the house to change for dinner.

Inevitably he either came back so late that she could wait no longer but was forced to go upstairs to have her bath, or else when he arrived it would be with one of his special friends like Peter Lansdown.

Sorilda suspected that Peter Lansdown was the only one of the Earl's friends to whom he had told the truth, and today, having tidied herself and washed her hands for luncheon, she went down to the Dining-Room to find, to her surprise, that he was there.

"Mr. Lansdown!" she exclaimed, and there was no mistaking the astonishment in her voice.

"Did Sholto not tell you to expect me?" he asked.

She shook her head.

"Sholto and I are having luncheon here today," Peter Lansdown explained, "because we have to be at the Crystal Palace at two o'clock. It is more convenient and nearer than lunching at White's."

"Of course, I understand," Sorilda said with a smile. "I am delighted to see you."

She liked Peter Lansdown and she knew, without his telling her so, that he admired her and there was no mistaking the expression in his eyes now as he looked at her new gown.

It was pale gold, the colour of daffodils, and Sorilda had thought it was one of the prettiest day-gowns she had ever seen.

She also had a larger crinoline than she had ever worn before. The dress-maker had in fact told her that they were getting bigger and bigger in Paris, so that Ladies of Fashion would soon require a whole carriage to themselves!

"You are very smart," Peter Lansdown said, "and, may I add without sounding impertinent, very beautiful."

"Thank you," Sorilda said, smiling.

Compliments no longer made her feel shy as they had at first, but instead evoked a little glow in her heart because she had been so long without them.

"I have a feeling," Peter Lansdown went on, "that when you appear at the inauguration of the Great Exhibition, looking as you do, you will outshine everyone present, and even the Queen will be jealous."

"I hope not," Sorilda said. "I admire the Queen and I am so delighted that the Palace is nearly finished and so far has not fallen down!"

Peter Lansdown laughed.

"Despite all the gloomy prophecies! I can assure you that Prince Albert is extremely grateful to everyone who, like Sholto, has supported him through thick and thin, which at times has been unpleasantly thick."

Sorilda had read the newspapers and she knew that

the protests about the Crystal Palace had not died down but rather accentuated during these last weeks.

The fact that the Great Exhibition was an advertisement for free trade infuriated the Protectionists, the "Fashionables," and the "fox-hunters" from the shires led by Colonel Sibthorp, who called down curses from Heaven upon this new Babel.

The foreign exhibitors were being denounced as a source of plague, political agitation, and crime.

Sorilda had heard someone say at dinner, when they thought the Earl was not listening, that England was now "inviting vipers into her bosom."

She had also learnt that the British Ambassador in Russia had reported to the Prime Minister that the Tzar had refused passports to the Russian nobility for fear of "contamination" in London.

She had read that not a single Crowned Head in Europe trusted himself under Prince Albert's glass roof, for a passport to England was too obviously a passport to eternity!

Peter Lansdown looked at his watch and said:

"Sholto's late, and I know why!"

"Why?" Sorilda enquired, knowing that he expected her to ask the question.

"Lord John Russell announced this morning," he replied, "that he objects to the arranged salute of guns north of the Serpentine, as he thinks it will shatter the crystal dome."

"Oh no!" Sorilda exclaimed.

"He wants the guns to be fired as far away as St. James's Park," Peter Lansdown continued, "but Sholto says it is nonsense and I agree with him."

As he spoke, the door opened and the Earl came in.

"Good-morning, Sorilda," he said as he walked towards them. "I have settled it, Peter!"

"How?" Peter Lansdown asked.

"I have told Lord John that no glass will break however much noise the guns make, and any piece that is cracked I will replace at my own expense."

Sorilda gave a little cry.

"But suppose the whole dome is damaged, it would cost you a fortune!"

"I will not be required to produce a penny-piece!" the Earl said firmly.

Because it was the first luncheon she had had with the Earl since they had driven away from the Castle after their wedding, and also the first meal at which there had not been a crowd of other guests, Sorilda enjoyed it enormously.

She listened to the Earl and Peter Lansdown teasing each other, capping each other's jokes, and arguing over the Crystal Palace in a way that she found fascinating, although she kept telling herself that her husband was despicable.

She was also sure that however busy he was, he still found time for a number of lady-loves!

When luncheon was over and the Earl and Peter Lansdown hurried off to Hyde Park, she found herself wishing wistfully that she could have gone with them.

She was longing to see this amazing Exhibition which had caused so much controversy, and to which despite their disapproval the newspapers had to devote page after page in describing what was occurring on the much-argued site in Hyde Park.

Despite all the gloomy predictions that it would never be finished, it was almost ready and Sorilda knew that it would be impossible not to admire the mere effort of covering over eighteen acres of ground and enclosing with glass thirty-three million cubic feet of space.

'I wish they had taken me with them,' she thought a little sadly as she went upstairs to her bedroom.

But then as she put on one of her new attractive bonnets she remembered that there was a great deal more shopping to do! The carriage and Mrs. Dawson would be waiting for her and that was an excitement in itself.

The following day, April 30, was one of showers. Once again they were giving a large dinner-party, and the Earl greeted his guests in an exceptionally good humour, telling them that the nineteen verses of Thackeray's *May Day Ode* had just been published.

"What does it say?" everyone asked.

The Earl read aloud the first four lines:

> "But yesterday a naked sod
>   The dandies sneered from Rotten Row
> And centered o'er it to and fro:
>   And see 'tis done!"

"Is it really done?" Sorilda asked.

"Completely finished," the Earl replied, "and tomorrow you will see for yourself that the Prince was justified in his conception of a Palace made of glass."

When their last guests left in the early hours of the morning, the Earl said:

"Are you looking forward to tomorrow?"

"More than I can tell you," Sorilda replied. "I have heard so much about the Palace and I have longed to accompany you when you have gone there nearly every day. So now it will be a terrible anticlimax if it is disappointing."

"I never thought of you accompanying me," the Earl replied with an air of surprise. "I could easily have taken you with me if you had told me you would have liked to come."

She did not answer and he went on:

"But I am sure you will not be disappointed. To me, not only was the whole conception brilliant, but the Exhibition comes up to my highest expectations of what it should be like."

Sorilda smiled and said:

"I think you really want it to be a success not only because you have supported the Prince all along, but because you think it will really help this country."

"That is right," the Earl said. "I do think it is important for England to show the world what she can do, and I am certain that the French and a great many other countries will be biting their nails with envy and jealousy after tomorrow."

Sorilda walked towards the stairs, then realised that the Earl had not followed her but was taking his hat from the hands of a flunkey.

"Are you going out?" she asked in surprise.

"You doubtless think me sentimental and unnecessarily apprehensive," he said, "but I am just going to drive to the Crystal Palace to see if it is still standing and make sure that the guards are alert to any damage which might be done at the last moment."

He smiled as he finished speaking, almost as if he mocked at himself, and then as he went through the front door to where the carriage was waiting for him, Sorilda went rather forlornly up the stairs alone to her own room.

"Why could I have not gone with him?" she asked herself.

Then she wondered if perhaps he was not going alone but intended to pick up one of his lady-loves to accompany him.

She gave a little sigh.

"If I minded, it would be agony to live with such a man," she told herself, then got into bed.

As she shut her eyes she deliberately concentrated on the gown she was to wear the following day!

* * *

"The sun's out, M'Lady!" her maid exclaimed almost ecstatically as she called Sorilda the following morning.

Sorilda sat up in bed.

"Oh! I am glad!" she said. "It would be too disappointing if it had rained and the Queen had had to drive to the Exhibition in a closed carriage."

When she came downstairs just before ten o'clock, she could already hear the peals of bells sounding from the steeples of every Church in London.

Mr. Barnham with his usual efficiency had told her that the Earl would be waiting for her in the Hall.

He looked up as Sorilda descended the stairs and she thought that he could not fail to admire her appearance.

Her dress was almost a poem of beauty with its huge crinoline of pale green silk, the colour of the buds of spring, with a bonnet trimmed with tiny curly ostrich-feathers and a frill of soft lace to frame her face.

As she reached the foot of the stairs Sorilda looked at the Earl almost enquiringly, feeling that even though he disliked her he could not fail to say that she was dressed perfectly for such a great occasion.

But he did not say anything until they had seated themselves in the open carriage in which they had the privilege of driving along the Royal Route to the Exhibition.

As they set off Sorilda forgot about herself because as soon as they reached the Park, she saw that on the branch of almost every tree there were small boys determined to have a good view.

There were over half-a-million people already assembled in the Park, and as Sorilda looked round her with delight at the colourful picture they made in the sunshine, she heard the Earl say:

"I see you are wearing my mother's emeralds."

She looked up at him quickly, aware that his eyes were on the necklace, the huge gems that fell from her small ears, and the bracelet to match, which she wore outside her left glove.

"Do you mind?" she enquired.

"They become you," he answered.

She thought this was the first compliment he had ever paid her.

Now they had their first glimpse of the flags of all nations which fluttered in the distance, but there were other things to see first: the model Frigate *Prince of Wales,* floating on the Serpentine, its crew at the ready to fire a salute, while Charles Spencer, the celebrated aeronaut, stood beside the basket of his balloon, ready to ascend the instant the Exhibition was declared open.

Now they joined a great number of other carriages travelling towards the Crystal Palace.

The Times had already told Sorilda, so that she had no need to ask the question, that over thirty thousand privileged guests with special tickets were to assemble to greet the Queen.

At last she could see the huge building glistening in the sunshine so that it seemed almost dazzling. Although she and the Earl were early, the inside of the huge space under the dome seemed to be filled with Diplomats, Officers of State, and other Court Dignitaries in gold-embroidered uniforms, all of them hurrying to their special places.

There was so much to look at, so much to see, that Sorilda felt she had little time to take in everything before the Gentlemen-at-Arms in their golden helmets, with long white plumes drooping over them, took their places at the back and sides of the throne.

Beside these were the portly-looking Beefeaters in their red suits and black velvet caps, and near them the trumpeters in gold coats with silver trumpets in their hands.

"They have arrived," Sorilda heard the Earl say quietly.

She had a glimpse through the glass of a troop of Life-Guards with their steel helmets and breast-plates glistening in the sunshine, and immediately afterwards there was the flourish of the trumpets which announced the arrival of the Queen.

Now for the first time Sorilda could see the young woman whom she had admired for so long. The Queen was wearing a dress of pink satin, sparkling with diamonds and silver, and was crowned with a tiara of diamonds and feathers.

She looked very small and yet very impressive as she walked beside Prince Albert, who was wearing the uniform of Field-Marshal. They were followed by the young Prince of Wales in Highland dress and the Princess Royal in a white dress with a wreath of roses in her hair.

There was a burst of cheering and then as the party stepped onto the dais the National Anthem was sung.

There were prayers and speeches and singing, and blasts from Henry Willis's Grand Organ. Then before the tour of inspection began, the Queen received those who had been responsible for the Exhibition, amongst them the Earl.

Their names were announced and as Sorilda curtseyed to the Queen, she heard Prince Albert say to the Earl:

"This is your triumph, My Lord, as well as mine. You were always so certain that it would be a success."

"As undoubtedly it is, Sire," the Earl said.

"You must congratulate the Earl of Winsford on his marriage, dearest," the Queen said to Prince Albert.

"I have already done so," Prince Albert replied, "but I want also to offer my good wishes to his wife."

He smiled at Sorilda as he spoke, and as she curtseyed she felt that his eyes rested on her in a kindly fashion.

"You must bring your wife to Buckingham Palace at the first opportunity, My Lord," the Queen said. "I will then have much more time than I have now in which to make her acquaintance."

"You are very gracious, Ma'am," the Earl replied.

Then as they moved aside so that other people could be presented, Sorilda saw someone watching her and realised with an unexpected tremor that it was her Step-aunt.

They were on the Royal Dais and the Duchess was looking lovely in blue, the colour of her eyes, and was ablaze with the Nuneaton diamonds.

There was an expression on her face, however, which made Sorilda feel as if cold steel were running down her back. Never had she seen such hatred in any woman's eyes, and she resisted an impulse to cling to the Earl as if asking him to save her.

But when they had moved away to follow in the Queen's wake and inspect the Exhibition, Sorilda could think of nothing but the wonders that were all round her.

There was so much to see that she felt breathless, and afterwards she found that her mind was a jumble of unrelated objects both large and small.

There was a monster block of coal weighing twenty-four tons from the Duke of Devonshire's Staverly Mines, a figure of Lazarus in artificial stone, and fountains from Austria, made of iron tubes.

Every nation had been allowed to display their different products as they pleased, and the elephant and houdah from India were as fascinating as the variety of smaller objects sent from America.

A sportsman's knife containing eighty blades amused the Earl, while a colossal porcelain vase from Russia had a crowd staring at it with open mouths.

Sorilda laughed at a collapsible piano for a gentleman's yacht and a pulpit which could be connected to the pews in Church by gutta-percha tubes for the use of the deaf.

But she was thrilled by the silks and satins from Lyons in France, the tapestries from the Gobelins and Beauvais work-shops, an enormous four-poster bed which the Earl told her had been purchased by the Queen, and the most attractive fans and mantillas from Spain.

"It is impossible to take in everything," she said excitedly to the Earl. "I shall have to come here every day until the Exhibition closes just in case I miss something."

She felt as she was speaking that her enthusiasm pleased him, and she thought it was difficult to go on being icily cold when she wanted to behave like a child at his first pantomime.

They walked so far and saw so much that she

had almost forgotten the Queen until the Earl hurried her to the exit to see the Royal Party leave.

To Sorilda's surprise, the Queen deliberately stopped to speak to her.

"I hope you have enjoyed the Exhibition, Lady Winsford."

"It is breathtaking, Ma'am."

"This is one of the greatest and most glorious days of my life," the Queen said with a smile, and there was no doubt that she spoke with complete sincerity.

As they drove away to the wild cheers of the crowd, Peter Lansdown joined Sorilda and the Earl.

"You are as puffed up with pride as a turkey-cock, Sholto," he teased. "And I have never seen the Prince look so pleased with himself."

"He has every right to be and so have I!" the Earl retorted. "We have worked like slaves to get everything completed."

"I must congratulate you too," said a voice which Sorilda knew only too well, and she saw that her Step-aunt was at the Earl's side.

"Thank you," the Earl replied gravely.

"It is always a joy when one's fondest desires are fulfilled," the Duchess said softly.

Sorilda was well aware that there was a hidden meaning to the words, and because she thought that the manner in which her Step-aunt had joined the Earl was outrageous, she deliberately walked away.

She had seen her Uncle in the distance, deep in conversation with Lord Aberdeen.

"I have just told Her Majesty," he was saying to the Duke, "that I do not remember anything before with which everyone was pleased as is the case with this Exhibition."

Knowing that he had decried it from its inception, Sorilda could not help wondering what the Duke would say, but before he was forced to answer, he saw her.

"Sorilda!" he exclaimed. "I saw the Queen

speaking to you. It was extremely gracious of Her Majesty and I am sure you felt honoured by her condescension."

"Of course I was, Uncle Edmund, and I was so delighted actually to see the Queen. It was something I was afraid would never happen."

The Duke looked uncomfortable.

"You should have been presented this year," he said gruffly, "but never mind. Now, I am sure, you will be continually invited to Buckingham Palace."

Sorilda wondered if she should remind him that she might have had a very different fate if she had remained at the Castle, but she thought it would be unkind. Instead she said:

"I think everything here is very wonderful and I hope I shall have more time another day to see everything, especially the agricultural-machinery, which I know must have especially interested you!"

It did not in fact interest Sorilda at all, but she felt that somehow she must hold her Uncle's attention and prevent him from realising how his wife was behaving.

"Yes, indeed," the Duke said at once, "I shall have to come and see them on my own when I next come to London. We are returning to the Castle tomorrow morning."

"Perhaps we could come here together, Uncle Edmund?" Sorilda said, and knew as he smiled at her that he was pleased at the suggestion.

Then the Duchess joined them.

"I was waiting for you to take me home," she said sharply to the Duke.

He looked at her and his eyes were cold.

"I will do so when I am ready," he answered.

Sorilda saw the Duchess press her lips together as if she longed to snap back at the rebuke.

Instead she looked at her Step-niece, and the anger that had been in her eyes when she watched her talking to the Queen was still there.

"I consider you overdressed," she said spitefully, "and you are wearing far too many jewels for a young woman!"

"You forget," Sorilda replied, "I am now a married woman, and my husband would expect me to put on a display to match the importance of the occasion."

She saw the anger flame like a fire into the Duchess's eyes before she turned away and went to where she saw the Earl was waiting for her with Peter Lansdown beside him.

She wondered what he had said to the Duchess to make her leave to rejoin the Duke, but she knew that that was a question she could not ask, and meekly she moved out through the main door to where their carriage was waiting.

Peter Lansdown drove with them and only as they reached Winsford House did the Earl say:

"I have to go down to the country tomorrow for a few days. Do you wish to accompany me?"

"Yes, of course," Sorilda said quickly.

She had no desire to stay alone in London, and she thought too that it would obviously create gossip if they were separated so soon after their marriage.

"Peter is coming with us," the Earl continued. "I want his advice on the work that is being done on the stables."

"Are you thinking of buying some new horses?" Sorilda enquired.

"I have, as a matter of fact, bought four this week," the Earl replied, "and I would like to see them comfortably installed. Could you be ready to leave by eleven o'clock?"

"Of course," Sorilda replied.

He said no more, and when they arrived at Winsford House he and Peter Lansdown, instead of joining Sorilda as she had expected in the Dining-Room, went into the Library. It was the Earl's special room, and she knew that she was not expected to intrude.

As she went upstairs to take off her bonnet and get ready for luncheon she found herself thinking of the Exhibition and hoping that they would return from the country soon so that she could go and see a great deal more of it.

Then she suddenly remembered that her Uncle had said that he and the Duchess were returning home to the Castle, and for the first time it suddenly struck her that that might be the reason why the Earl had decided to go to Winsford Park.

"Surely he does not intend to continue his liaison with my Step-aunt now that we are married?" she asked herself.

It seemed incredible, and yet Iris had deliberately sought him out at the Exhibition. Perhaps she had told him that they were returning to the country and so the Earl had made up his mind to return to Winsford Park himself.

"How dare he do such a thing! How dare Iris continue to be unfaithful to Uncle Edmund!"

To Sorilda it was sordid to the point of being disgusting as well as degrading.

"I will not go! I will stay here and let them do what they like!" she exclaimed.

Then she knew that it would be a mistake to let herself become isolated with only her resentment and anger to keep her company.

Besides, her supposition might be entirely false. It seemed inconceivable that, having been caught out once in pursuit of his neighbour's wife, the Earl should risk disclosure for the second time.

'It must be just coincidence that we are going to Winsford Park when Uncle Edmund and Iris will be at the Castle,' Sorilda thought.

But the suspicion was there in her mind, and later as she looked at the Earl at the end of the table she felt an almost irresistible impulse to ask if what she suspected was true.

Then she knew that it would be a foolish thing to do and might cause her humiliation. What could she say if he replied that he loved Iris too much to give her up?

How could he really like anyone so shallow and so unpleasant as the Duchess? Then Sorilda knew that whatever her character might be, Iris had looked almost breathtakingly beautiful at the opening of the Exhibition.

How was the Earl to know that while she was all sweetness and charm to him, beneath her lovely exterior she was viperish, spiteful, and cruel?

'He would not believe me if I told him,' Sorilda thought helplessly.

Then Peter Lansdown said something to make her laugh and for the moment she forgot the feelings of disgust that seemed once again to discolour everything, even her dreams.

Chapter Six

"I will leave you to your port."

Sorilda rose from the Dining-Room table as she spoke, and as the Earl and Peter Lansdown rose too, she smiled at them and walked towards the door.

There was a scrabble from under the table and a brown and white spaniel hurried after her.

As they both left the room, Peter Lansdown said to the Earl:

"I notice that Drake follows your wife everywhere."

"As he used to follow me!" the Earl replied. "So much for loyalty from what is called 'man's best friend'!"

"He has certainly now become a woman's most ardent admirer!" Peter Lansdown said with a smile as he reseated himself at the table. "And he is not the only one."

The Earl glanced at him sharply.

"What do you mean by that remark?"

"Merely that with your usual astounding luck, Sholto, and in the most unlikely circumstances, you have found a wife who is exceptional in every way."

The Earl did not reply and Peter Lansdown went on:

"Sorilda is not only extremely beautiful and very intelligent, she rides superbly, and already has every-

121

one on your estate eating out of her hand, while your dog never leaves her side."

The Earl, with some deliberation, poured himself another glass of port and passed the decanter to his friend.

"I admit," he said after a moment in a carefully restrained voice, "that things might have been worse."

"Good God! That is indeed to 'damn with faint praise,' " Peter Lansdown quoted. "You have scooped the pool, won the Cup, carried home a trophy of inestimable value, and you say things might have been worse!"

He laughed and went on:

"Well, as I have already warned you, Drake is not Sorilda's only admirer, and I predict that you will soon have to look to your laurels or she will fall into the arms of someone more reponsive."

"Yourself for instance!" the Earl said in a sour tone.

"I had thought of it," Peter Lansdown replied, "and I can tell you, Sholto, it is only because I am your friend and value our friendship that I have not made an advance in that direction."

The Earl stared for a moment in speechless astonishment, then said angrily:

"Damn it all! You have no right to speak to me in that manner! You know the circumstances in which I was pressured into marriage, and it is not something I can forget in a hurry!"

"That was hardly Sorilda's fault. In fact, if she had not saved you in what I consider a very generous manner, you might have found yourself in a much more uncomfortable situation. After all, the Duke has a great deal of influence with the Queen."

The Earl did not speak and Peter Lansdown went on:

"I do not suppose you would consider it comfortable to be exiled for some years and have your new Garter and a great many other decorations taken from you."

"For God's sake, shut up!" the Earl retorted. "I am sick of the subject. I . . ."

He was about to say something else when a servant entered the room. He walked to the Earl's side carrying a silver salver on which reposed a note.

The Earl looked at it and stiffened.

"A groom is waiting, M'Lord."

"There will be no answer!"

The servant bowed and went from the room.

The Earl sat staring at the note in his hand without making any effort to open it.

"The Duchess?" Peter Lansdown questioned.

"Who else!" the Earl replied savagely. "What the hell am I to do with the woman? She never leaves me alone!"

"Poor Sholto," Peter Lansdown said mockingly. "I cannot help being sorry for you. You leave London to avoid Alison Fane and find an importunate Duchess waiting for you in the country!"

Taking the note, the Earl reached out and held the corner of it to one of the candles in the gold candelabra. When it was well alight he put it down on his empty plate and let it burn itself to ash.

"I am beginning to realise," he said slowly, "that the Duchess is one of those women who fasten onto one like a leach, and I have always had a vast distaste for the species."

"I am really rather sorry for you," Peter Lansdown said in a different tone. "At the same time, do not neglect Sorilda for too long, and I mean that in all sincerity."

"What are you trying to say to me?" the Earl asked irritably.

Peter Lansdown sat back in his chair, his glass of port in his hand.

"She is like the Sleeping Beauty," he ruminated, "young, sweet, and innocent. I am just wondering who will be the first person to awaken her."

"If you try to seduce my wife, I will call you out!" the Earl snapped.

"I am nearly as good a shot as you are," Peter Lansdown replied, "and actually it might be worth it!"

"I think you have gone mad!" the Earl stormed. "And let me remind you in no uncertain terms, Sorilda is married to me!"

"Legally, yes!"

There was silence and then Peter Lansdown added:

"Wrothan said to me before we left London that she was the most entrancing creature on whom he had ever set eyes. I am sure he is only waiting for her return to tell her so."

The Earl's lips tightened and Peter Lansdown glanced at him swiftly before he continued:

"I had a feeling that Chester also was pursuing her. He certainly danced with her no less than three times at the Richmonds' Ball. So perhaps she fancies him."

The Earl rose to his feet.

"Stop! I do not intend to discuss my wife with anyone, not even you, and as it is a warm evening I suggest that before we join Sorilda we walk to the stables. Roxana produced a foal today which I am told is quite outstanding. I have not yet had time to see it."

"I am certain Sorilda will understand why she has to wait for us," Peter Lansdown said sarcastically as he finished his port.

He was well aware that the Earl was scowling as he walked towards the door, but his own eyes were twinkling and the smile on his lips was that of a man who thinks he has been exceptionally clever.

*   *   *

Sorilda, having left the Dining-Room, found one of the footmen waiting in the Hall with three other spaniels which belonged to the Earl.

"I expect you are waiting for Drake, Henry."

"Yes, M'Lady."

"I did not realise he had slipped into the Dining-Room with me. It is naughty of him when he knows it is time for his evening walk."

"He hates t' be away from you, M'Lady."

"He knows I love him," Sorilda said, smiling.

It had in fact been an inexpressible pleasure to have a dog of her own. Her Uncle would never allow dogs inside the Castle and his game-dogs were confined to the kennels.

Although Sorilda had regularly visited them, it had not been the same as having a dog who followed her everywhere and slept beside her bed at night.

From the moment they had arrived over a week ago at Winsford Park, Drake had attached himself to her, despite the Earl's surprise. Sorilda sometimes thought he was piqued that one of his own dogs should desert him so obviously.

But when the Earl was busy, or when he and Peter Lansdown went off somewhere together, because Drake was with her Sorilda no longer felt alone or lonely.

She bent down now to pat him.

"Go for a nice walk with Henry," she said, "and another time do not play truant under the Dining-Room table!"

She laughed as she spoke, and Henry, who was a country-boy, whistled between his teeth as he walked across the Hall and out through the front door, followed by the four dogs, wagging their tails.

Sorilda went into the Dining-Room and thought how in the last week she was happier than she had been in many years.

Everything about Winsford Park was so beautiful, the house, its contents, its surroundings, and most of all the thrill she experienced every time she was allowed to ride the Earl's horses.

This morning she had raced him and Peter Lansdown down the Long Gallop and had nearly beaten them.

As she did so, she remembered how so recently

she had peeped at the Earl from beneath the branches of the trees.

Never in her wildest dreams would she have believed that she would become the wife of the man who rode so magnificently on such outstanding horse-flesh.

She thought with a sigh that they would be forced to leave Winsford Park soon. The Earl not only had commitments at the House of Lords, but Prince Albert would expect him to be seen frequently at the Crystal Palace.

She knew that once they left the quiet of the country there would be parties, Balls, and Receptions every night, and it would be impossible to talk to the Earl or to listen to him as she was able to do now.

Although she told herself that she still despised him and thought his behaviour outrageous, it was impossible to keep up her poise of icy disdain when there were so many exciting things to do and so many interesting things to discuss.

Now she had the chance of learning a great deal about the political situation and the fears of French aggression, which the Earl told her was being discussed in secret by the Cabinet.

Sorilda had always thought that politics could be fascinating, and as she plied the Earl with questions she could not help thinking that in a way he seemed rather pleased to be able to air his views to an audience which, if small, was very receptive.

She was glad too that Peter Lansdown was staying at Winsford Park.

She thought he made the Earl far more human and less awe-inspiring because he teased him and often laughed away the irritation in his voice and the frown between his eyes.

"He is also very kind to me," Sorilda told herself.

She had known, after no more than two or three days at Winsford Park, that everything was easier and a great deal happier than she had ever expected, because he was there.

The weather was getting warm and in fact the newspapers said it was an exceptional May.

Sorilda also learnt from the Society-columns of *The Times* that the London Season was in full swing, and because of the Exhibition there were more Balls and parties than there had been in many years.

It seemed strange, she thought, that the Earl, who, Mr. Barnham had told her, had more invitations than anyone he had ever known, wished to stay in the country.

She found herself wondering if it had anything to do with her Step-aunt, but the Earl never mentioned her and there was no obvious communication between Winsford Park and the Castle.

"Thank goodness for that!" Sorilda said in the privacy of her own bedroom.

She had not forgotten the expression in the Duchess's eyes at the opening of the Exhibition, and she supposed that she was sitting at the Castle hating her with every breath that she drew, because she was married to the man on whom she had set her heart.

'I suppose really I should be sorry for her,' Sorilda thought, 'but I am not! She married Uncle Edmund and she should try to be happy with him. He adores her, or did until this happened.'

She wondered what it would be like to be adored by one's husband, and sometimes when her thoughts ran away with her, she found herself wondering what the Earl had said to her Step-aunt when he made love to her.

Also what he had done to make Lady Alison so fanatically obsessed with him.

"No man should be so good-looking," she murmured now. "It is not fair to foolish women who lose their hearts so easily!"

She crossed the room to the window which opened onto a terrace with a stone balustrade which ran along that side of the house with covered steps leading down into a formal garden laid out, the Earl had told her, like the garden at the Palace of Versailles.

The sun had already set behind the great trees in the Park, but the glow of it was still translucent in the sky. It was that breathless moment at dusk before the first stars come out and the last light of the day disappears.

It always seemed to Sorilda a moment when her heart seemed to soar out of her body and into a world which she sensed but could not see; a world in which she felt her mother was very near.

She moved onto the terrace, feeling that the beauty of everything enveloped her so that she became a part of it. Then unexpectedly, so that it made her start, she heard a faint sound from below her.

She looked over the balustrade and saw a small boy.

"Be ye th' Countess?" he asked.

"I am," Sorilda replied, "but who are you and what are you doing here?"

"Oi were t' tell ye t' come a' once!"

"But why?"

" 'Tis yer dog, 'e be 'urt."

"Drake? He has had an accident?" Sorilda exclaimed. "Where is he?"

"Oi'll take ye t' 'im."

She ran along the terrace and down the steps to find the boy waiting for her at their foot.

" 'Urry, Missus!"

Sorilda picked up her full skirts, holding on to the band of whalebone underneath so that she could move quickly. The boy was running ahead and it was difficult to keep up with him.

He ran through the formal garden and then turned behind a high yew-hedge which bordered one of the lawns, beyond which were the shrubberies.

As Sorilda followed, breathless from the speed at which the boy was running, she wondered what could have happened. It must be something serious for Henry to have to send the boy to fetch her.

They had gone some way before she wished

that she had waited and asked the Earl to come with her.

If Drake was hurt she was sure that he would know what to do. She had realised from their talks that he not only knew a great deal about horses but about dogs as well.

She remembered Huxley saying a long time ago:

"There's one thing, Miss Sorilda, about th' Earl, he don't just own his horses, he understands 'em, an' ye can't say that about every gentleman as takes home th' prizes!"

Sorilda had known that this was high praise from Huxley!

Ever since she had been married to the Earl she had realised that in fact he knew every detail about the horses he possessed, and when he visited the stables nothing escaped his critical eye.

'Drake is hurt and he will know how to cure him,' she thought, and wondered how much farther she would have to go to find the dog.

It was almost dark in the shrubbery as they passed through it and then Sorilda saw silhouetted against the darkening sky the ruins of the old Abbey.

When the original Winsford Park had been built in the fifteenth century it had been a large and flourishing Monastery, only to fall into disuse after Henry VIII's dissolution of the Monasteries.

The ruins of the Abbey in which the Monks had worshipped could still be seen. The roof had gone but three walls remained, and when the Earl had shown it to Sorilda when they were riding, she had thought it very romantic.

"It is a beauty spot," he had said with a smile, "and the fact that it attracts a number of visitors infuriates my keepers, who say they interfere with the game in the woods, and my gardeners, who say they make the place untidy."

"I can understand people wanting to come here,"

Sorilda had replied. "It is very attractive, and I feel it still has an air of sanctuary about it."

"Sorilda's right," Peter Lansdown had said, "and if you were the Churchman you ought to be, Sholto, you would rebuild it and let people worship here as they used to do."

"That is something I have no intention of doing," the Earl had replied firmly. "Besides, as you well know, there is nothing young women enjoy more than ruins, usually painting them excruciatingly badly in sloppy water-colours!"

He had spoken in such a disparaging way that both Peter Lansdown and Sorilda had burst out laughing.

"I promise you," she had said, "I will not paint the ruins, and I dislike water-colours!"

"You should be grateful," Peter Lansdown had said to the Earl, "that you will not have to frame Sorilda's efforts!"

"There will be no water-colours in any house I own!" the Earl had declared positively, and Peter Lansdown had laughed and teased him for being unfashionable.

It only took the small boy a few more minutes to reach the ruins, but by now Sorilda was very breathless.

"Where is . . . Drake? Where is . . . he?" she asked, gasping.

There was nothing to see except the broken walls, as they pushed through the bushes just coming into leaf which had grown all over what had once been the main aisle of the Abbey.

" 'E's here!" the boy replied, pointing to the ground.

Sorilda moved to his side in astonishment and saw that he was pointing at some rough steps that went straight down into the earth.

For a moment she stared incredulously, then she understood! This was the old crypt of the Abbey, and Drake, for some extraordinary reason, must have fallen down the steps into it.

She looked into the dark hole and realised that at the bottom there was a faint light.

"Is Drake down there?" she asked. "And where is Henry and the other dogs?"

The boy did not answer but merely pointed, and because Sorilda felt there was nothing further he could do, she lifted her gown a little higher and started to climb rather gingerly down the steps.

She went down backwards as if she were in a yacht, holding on to the two steps above her.

It was difficult to do because she was encumbered by her crinoline, and the steps, rough and worn with age, were uneven. Feeling with her foot each time before she went lower, Sorilda finally reached the ground.

She looked up to see the small boy's head silhouetted against the sky as he peered down at her. Then she turned and saw that she had not been mistaken in thinking that there was a light.

It was some way inside the crypt and she walked towards it, feeling apprehensively that Drake must have been carried away from the steps down which he had fallen, presumably to a place where Henry could lay him down and see how badly he was hurt.

"Perhaps he has broken a leg, in which case he will be in considerable pain," she told herself.

The floor of the crypt was covered with flat flagstones and it was easy now for her to move quickly, and when she passed a pillar of bricks she could see the candle.

It was stuck on the floor, but surprisingly in the area it illuminated there was nothing to be seen!

Sorilda looked round in astonishment. There was no Drake, no Henry, and none of the other dogs she had expected to find.

"Henry, where are you?"

Her voice seemed to echo strongly and rather

eerily round the empty crypt and return to her like a ghostly echo.

"Henry! Drake!"

She suddenly thought that if Drake were alive and conscious, he, at any rate, would respond to her voice.

"Drake! Drake!" she called, but there was only silence.

She shouted the names of the other dogs:

"Nelson! Roger! Royal!"

It was frightening to hear her own voice echoing and re-echoing, and then she knew that there was no-one in the crypt except herself.

She supposed that after Henry had sent the boy to fetch her, he had managed to carry Drake up the steps. Doubtless by this time he was back at the house and they had missed each other.

It was agitating to wonder exactly what had happened, but she supposed Henry had panicked when the accident had first happened. After he had sent for her, he must have realised that he could manage quite competently on his own.

'I shall find Drake at home,' Sorilda thought, 'and the sooner I get back, the better.'

She reached the bottom of the steps and looked up, expecting to see the boy's head silhouetted against the sky.

Then she realised that there was no sky but something dark and solid in its place. It took her a few seconds to realise that what she was looking at was the cover of the crypt—two iron doors which had been open when she had descended the steps but which now were closed.

'How extraordinary,' she thought.

"Open the doors!" she shouted. "I am coming up!"

There was no reply, and she started to clamber up the steps, finding it, despite the crinoline, easier going up than it had been going down.

Five steps brought her head almost against the iron doors.

"Open these doors!" she ordered, and as she did so she put up her right hand to push against one of them.

It was cold and very solid. She pushed harder, holding on to the top step firmly with her left hand.

Then quite suddenly she realised that whatever strength she tried to exert was useless. The crypt doors had been closed and she was certain, having seen a crypt before, that there was a strong bolt which held them in place.

For some seconds Sorilda stood where she was, her head thrown upwards. Then very slowly she descended the steps again to stand on the floor of the crypt.

What was happening?

Why had she been brought here?

Where was Drake?

Then she knew as clearly as if someone had told her. There had been no accident, and she was a prisoner in the crypt!

It might be a long time before anyone found her!

Because the idea was so terrifying, she walked back to the candle and looked at it apprehensively.

It was a small candle and must have already been burning for quite a long while. When it burnt itself out she would be in darkness!

Horrified at the thought, Sorilda shouted frantically:

"Help! Help!"

But there was only the echo as the walls seemed to bring her voice back to her.

"Help! Help!"

'I must not panic!' she thought. 'I must think sensibly of what I can do, how I can escape.'

The words seemed to make her remember how desperately she had wanted to escape from the Castle, only now to be a prisoner in the crypt of a ruined Abbey!

"Someone will find me," she told herself, "but how soon?"

The Earl had said there were often visitors to the ruins. It was still early in the year for picnickers and she had an uncomfortable feeling that what he thought of as being a lot of visitors might consist of perhaps only two or three small parties a month.

She drew in her breath. If she stayed here long, she could easily die without food, without light, and with the cold.

Even as she thought of it she shivered. She had been so anxious to find Drake that it never struck her how cold it was as she climbed down into the crypt.

But now, incarcerated below ground, she could feel the chill of the stone floors rising as if to suck the warmth of her body from her.

"Help! Help!"

In a panic which she could not control, she rushed back to the steps and, climbing up them, pushed with every ounce of her strength against the closed iron doors.

It was hopeless, completely hopeless! And now she was afraid with a fear which seemed to rise within her breasts like an evil serpent.

"No-one will find me and I shall die here alone. Oh! Sholto, save me!"

Even as she called out for the Earl in a voice which was little above a whisper, she knew why she was imprisoned.

It was the Duchess who had translated her hatred into action and who had brought her here to die!

The Duchess, who wanted the Earl to be free of her, had thought out this diabolical plan to further her own ends and her own desires!

Sorilda climbed down the steps and, sitting on them, put her hands up to her face.

"What shall I do?" she asked herself. "O God, help me! What shall I do?"

* * *

The Earl walked into the Hall, followed by Peter Lansdown. They both looked tired almost to the point of exhaustion.

As the Butler hurried forward the Earl said:

"Bring something to eat immediately and order fresh horses in half-an-hour's time!"

"Very good, M'Lord. Will you have something to drink in the Library?"

"Brandy!" the Earl replied.

"It's there, M'Lord."

The Butler hurried to open the Library door.

The Earl walked into the room and flung himself down on one of the chairs beside the fireplace.

Peter Lansdown stood for a moment, brushing back his hair from his forehead, before he collapsed into another chair, his legs stuck out in front of him.

They took the glasses of brandy the Butler offered them.

"Will you be changing in any way, M'Lord?"

"No, I will dine as I am," the Earl replied, "and so will Mr. Lansdown."

When the Butler had left the room, the Earl said:

"Where else can we look? I think yesterday and today we must have covered the whole of the estate."

"You still do not think that she has run away?"

"In only what she stood up in?"

"We have discussed all this before," Peter Lansdown said. "She was definitely not unhappy. She seemed amused at everything we said at dinner that night, and there was no way of her leaving the house except on foot."

The Earl drank some of his brandy before he said:

"You will laugh at me, but I have a feeling that something terrible—almost evil—has happened. I cannot explain it, but all the time it is there in my mind."

Peter Lansdown looked at him in surprise.

"What could it be?" he asked.

"I do not know! If I did, I would have done something about it, but I just do not know. We must find Sorilda, and something tells me it must be quickly!"

Peter Lansdown gave a little gesture of hopelessness. All the previous day he and the Earl had ridden over the grasslands, through the woods, visiting every farm and almost every cottage on the vast estate.

The keepers and the woodsmen were searching too, once the Earl had decided that he must announce that the Countess had disappeared.

When the Earl and Peter Lansdown had gone into the Dining-Room after visiting the stables, it was to find it empty, and the Earl had supposed that Sorilda had gone to bed.

It was only very much later that night that he had heard a dog scratching and whining and wondered why.

He thought at first that it was one of his own dogs who slept with him, but then he realised that the sound was not in his room but in Sorilda's, next door.

He knew that Drake was with her and thought it strange that the dog should be behaving in such a manner and that she made no effort to rebuke him.

The Earl lay listening to the sound for some time and then decided that something must be wrong.

Feeling slightly embarrassed in case Sorilda thought he was intruding on her, he got out of bed, put on his robe, and went to the communicating-door which stood between their bedrooms.

He knocked, and instantly Drake stopped whining and gave a bark.

"Are you awake, Sorilda?"

There was no answer and this time Drake barked more loudly. The Earl tried the door but it was locked. He opened the door into the corridor and went to the other door of Sorilda's room.

Now Drake had resumed his scratching and whining until as the Earl opened the door the dog rushed at him, jumping in wild excitement at his appearance.

"What is it, old boy?" the Earl asked. "What has upset you?"

He looked towards the bed. The candles were lit and he could see that the bed had not been slept in, and Sorilda's nightgown was lying with her dressing-gown on a chair.

The Earl was bewildered, finding it difficult to understand what had happened. Then he went back to his own room and rang the bell.

It was some time before he could ascertain from his valet, who awakened the Housekeeper, who roused Sorilda's lady's-maid, that the Countess had not rung her bell to be helped out of her gown.

In fact, no-one upstairs in the house had heard from her since she had gone down to dinner.

The Earl had searched the whole house with the Night-watchmen and when it was dawn he had awakened Peter Lansdown.

"The French window in the Dining-Room was open," the Earl said. "I can only imagine that she went out into the garden for a walk and has had an accident. We will start searching, and I will send one of the footmen to wake the gardeners."

Though they had spent the whole of that day looking for Sorilda, there was no sign of her.

It had been the same today, and Peter Lansdown had known when they exchanged their exhausted horses at luncheon-time for two fresh ones, that the Earl was as tired as he was but neither of them intended to give in.

"Where the devil can she be?" the Earl asked now. "If there were quick-sands somewhere on the estate she might have fallen into them, but there is nothing like that, and as you know, the lake is not deep enough to drown anyone."

"Sorilda also told me she could swim. Is there a well that might be dangerous?" Peter Lansdown hazarded.

"If there is, I have never heard of it," the Earl answered. "The well we use for the house has a pumping-machine, so it would be impossible for anyone to drown in it without first moving the machinery."

"Then what . . . ?" Peter Lansdown began in a tired voice as the door opened and the Butler came to the Earl's side.

"Excuse me, M'Lord. But Betsy has asked if she could see you."

"Betsy!" the Earl enquired.

"She's one of the maids who work in the kitchen, M'Lord. She says she's something she must tell Your Lordship personally, and I fancy it's to do with Her Ladyship."

"Send her in," the Earl said quickly.

"Very good, M'Lord."

The Butler withdrew and Peter Lansdown rose slowly to his feet.

"I am going to wash," he said, "and I think you had better listen to this girl alone. She might be embarrassed if I am here too."

"I cannot think what on earth she has to say to me," the Earl replied.

"Any clue is better than none," Peter Lansdown said as he walked towards the door.

The Earl waited and it was some minutes before the Butler announced:

"Betsy, M'Lord."

The Earl watched Betsy come into the room. He saw that she was an attractive young woman of seventeen or eighteen, but because she was afraid, her face was very pale and she was twisting her fingers together over her white apron. She dropped a curtsey.

"Your name is Betsy?" the Earl asked in a quiet tone.

"Yes, M'Lord."

"I understand you have something to tell me."

"It mightn't help, M'Lord, but I thinks as how I ought t' tell Your Lordship."

"I shall be very grateful for anything that will help me find Her Ladyship. As you are well aware, she has disappeared in a most mysterious way, and I cannot help thinking that she has been involved in some accident."

"Yes, M'Lord, that's what they says in th' kitchen."

There was silence while Betsy was obviously groping for words, and the Earl said encouragingly:

"Tell me everything you can remember. One never knows what small thing might help."

"Yes, M'Lord. Well, th' night Her Ladyship disappeared, Jim brought a note for Your Lordship from th' Castle."

"Who is Jim?" the Earl asked.

"He's a groom at th' Castle, M'Lord, an' I've known him all my life—we're sweet on each other."

The words seemed to burst out apprehensively and the Earl was aware that Betsy looked at him in a frightened manner.

"I quite understand, Betsy. You are a very pretty girl and Jim obviously has good taste."

The words brought a faint smile to Betsy's lips, and the Earl prompted:

"Go on."

"After Jim'd been told there was no answer for him t' take back," Betsy said, "I walks wi' him down th' drive."

She twisted her fingers a little more vigorously as she said:

"We were rather a long time about it, M'Lord. We means t' get married one day when us has th' money."

"We must talk about that another time," the Earl said. "Perhaps I will be able to help you. Tell me now what happened."

"We gets near th' lodges, M'Lord, and sat there a little while, when suddenly we sees someone ridin' across th' fields t'wards us."

Betsy's voice trembled a little as she said:

"I knows I oughtn't be out so late, an' as we didna want anyone t' see us, Jim leads his horse behind a big rhododendron an' I hides wi' him."

"I am sure that was a sensible thing to do," the Earl said. "Who was on the horse?"

"That's what I were a-going t' tell you, M'Lord. He rides on t' th' drive an' then passes quite near t' us t' go through th' gates."

The Earl waited, his eyes on Betsy's face.

"Only when he were gone did I say t' Jim, 'That were Len!'

" 'Yes, Len,' Jim says, 'an' on one o' our horses. Oi don't know what Mr. Huxley'd say t' that.' "

"Who is Len?" the Earl asked, as if he could not wait for Betsy to keep to the story.

"That's what I were just about t' tell you, M'Lord. He's a new groom none o' us likes at th' Castle."

"You were at the Castle before you came here?"

"Yes, M'Lord, but Her Grace turned me off without a reference, cruel it was, an' almost broke me father an' mother's heart it did!"

"Tell me about Len," the Earl said.

"Len comes t' th' Castle with Her Grace. He's a neighbour o' her lady's-maid. They hates him in th' stables, 'cause they thinks he spies on 'em. He carries tales t' Miss Harriet, who tell 'em t' Her Grace."

"I think I understand what you are telling me," the Earl said slowly. "So Len is to all intents and purposes the Duchess's servant."

"Yes, M'Lord. An' it seems funny t' Jim and I that he should be about when Her Ladyship disappeared, knowin' as how Her Grace hates Miss Sorilda an'd do anythin' t' harm her if her could."

Betsy spoke spitefully and the Earl looked at her in astonishment.

"Are you suggesting," he asked, "that Len has something to do with Her Ladyship's disappearance?"

"I'd not be surprised," Betsy replied. "What were he a-doing there in th' first place an' riding a horse he'd no right t' take from th' stables?"

"I think I follow your reasoning," the Earl said.

"From what direction was Len coming when you saw him?"

"He were riding down the field th' other side o' th' shrubberies, M'Lord. I supposed 'twas from th' direction o' th' old Abbey."

"The old Abbey!" the Earl repeated.

"I've been there, M'Lord, an' ever so creepy it were, with all those broken walls, an' when I goes down into th' crypt I feels as if I were in me grave."

"The crypt!"

The Earl's voice seemed to ring out and he sprang to his feet.

"That is where we have not looked!" he exclaimed.

As he walked quickly towards the door, he said over his shoulder:

"Thank you, Betsy. If I find Her Ladyship, I promise that you can start planning your wedding!"

Chapter Seven

Sorilda awoke with a little start and realised that she had dozed off with her head against a brick pillar.

She had sat down so as to be near the candle, at the same time hoping vainly that it might give out a little heat to ease the cold which had seeped over her whole body until she felt as if she were enclosed in ice.

When her teeth began to chatter she pulled up her full skirt and covered her bare shoulders with it. As she did so, it struck her that she might be warmer if her petticoat was against her legs instead of over the whalebone of the crinoline.

She slipped off the frame and thought for a moment that the softness of the silk made her feel a little warmer. Then, wrapped in the skirt, she crossed her arms and sat down by the candle.

Now as she looked at it she noticed that the candle-wick was almost level with the ground and flickering in a manner which told her it would be only a few minutes or even seconds before it was extinguished.

Then she would be alone in the dark!

As she thought of it she glanced apprehensively into the shadows of the far walls, knowing that they contained the coffins of Monks who had died long ago.

"They will not hurt me," she told herself sensibly, "they are holy and they will protect me from evil."

143

But they had not been able to protect her against being imprisoned in the crypt on what she was certain was the Duchess's order.

No-one would find her and she would die slowly of cold and starvation until years later they would find only her bones rotting away in her silk evening-gown.

The thought of it made her want to scream. Then she told herself severely that this was the moment when she must pray for help and believe, even though it seemed unlikely, that her prayers would be heard.

Then as she started to pray she found that her whole being was crying out for the Earl. He was so strong, so athletic, and if anyone could rescue her it would be he.

She thought wildly that she did not care if he held a hundred other women in his arms as long as she could be close to him and he could extricate her from this cold, dark prison.

"I was meant to be a prisoner all my life," Sorilda whispered to herself with a little sob. "First a prisoner in the Castle and now a prisoner in a ruined crypt where no-one will think to look for me."

Then she suddenly realised that she was in yet another prison!

The mere idea of it made her stiffen. It could not be true!

What she was thinking must be the result of her fear and could not come to her mind for any other reason.

However, the more she protested, the more she knew that what she thought was true.

She loved the Earl!

It seemed incredible, since she had felt only disdain for him, but she knew now why she had been so happy these last few days when they had ridden together, when she had listened to him telling her what was happening in Parliament, and when she had heard him laughing with Peter Lansdown.

She loved him!

Then she told herself, helplessly, that it was inevitable that it should happen. What did she know about men, having been brought up in the Castle since her parents had died and seeing only her Uncle's contemporaries.

"I would have been abnormal if I had not fallen in love with the most attractive man in the world," she told herself. "And now I am a prisoner in love!"

She tried to laugh, but instead she only ached for the Earl, not only because she wanted him to save her but also because she wanted him as a man.

Many other women had wanted him in the same way, she told herself, but she still yearned for his arms round her, his lips against hers.

'Perhaps it would be better to die,' she thought.

It could be a worse agony to live beside him, knowing she wanted him as the Duchess did and Lady Alison and many others whose names she did not know.

Yet every instinct made her want to live!

She wanted to see the Earl again, to hear his voice, to see the twinkle in his eyes when something amused him, and to hear his laughter, which had something boyish about it.

"I am his wife! His wife!" Sorilda told herself.

But she thought despairingly that she was a wife only in name.

He had been so angry at having to marry her, and all she could remember was how when they had been in London he had never seemed to look at her and they had never been alone.

'Perhaps he feels a little ... differently about me now,' she thought.

But they would soon return to London and there would be other people for him to talk to, to dance with, and they would never be alone together.

Because he was not interested in her, she knew she would feel utterly lonely even in the most crowded room.

"I love him! I love him!" she cried aloud, and her teeth chattered as she did so.

She could feel the cold damp rising from the floor and she thought that perhaps she should get up and walk about, but even as she considered doing so, the candle gave a last flicker and went out.

Now the darkness was menacing and the ghosts of the Monks seemed to haunt her.

Perhaps too, she thought wildly, the evil emanating from the Duchess was there too and her Step-aunt would be chuckling because she had walked so easily into the trap that had been set for her.

"How could I have been such a fool?" Sorilda asked herself.

She wished as she had wished one hundred times already that she had run to the Dining-Room and told the Earl what had occurred.

'It is too late!' she thought again.

She would die here in the cold and he would never find her and would never know how much she loved him.

"I want you! I want you!" she called out in her heart.

She thought if only he had held her in his arms and perhaps kissed her just once, she could die happily.

Then her courage told her that happy or unhappy, she must struggle not to die.

She forced herself to stand up and to stamp her satin-slippered feet on the ground, with one hand holding on to the pillar in case she should get lost in the dark.

Then she sat down again to try to pray. . . .

* * *

A long, long time later, when Sorilda was shivering as if she had the ague, she walked with her hands outstretched in front of her in case she should bump into anything, and found her way to the steps.

She looked up and now she could see a faint line of light where the two iron doors joined, and she knew it must be daylight.

She listened, hoping that she might hear voices, but there was only very faintly the sound of the birds.

'If the birds are singing, there must be no-one there to frighten them,' Sorilda thought, and knew it would be hopeless to cry for help.

Because she hoped it might be a little warmer, she climbed a little way up the steps, but as she did so there was a sudden pattern of rain on the iron doors.

As she listened she felt as if the mere sound of the rain made her feel colder than she had been before.

She was not hungry, she merely felt empty inside, but as the hours passed she began to grow thirsty. She thought that even to drink rain-water would be better than nothing, but there was no chance of obtaining any.

Slowly, slowly time moved on, and now in a sudden terror and fear Sorilda cried for help, but again her voice only echoed round the darkness of the crypt and she knew that it would not carry far enough to attract attention.

Because it was so uncomfortable sitting on the steps, she went down on the floor and, creeping back to the pillar, sat with her back against it.

She tried to calculate how long it would take for her to die, but instead she found herself thinking of the Earl.

'Why of all men did he have to come into my life?' she wondered.

She had found herself remembering how he had looked when he had come into her bedroom at the Castle and seemed surprised to see her sitting up against her pillows, looking at him.

Then with a little throb of her heart she could remember the anger emanating from him when they had been married and the cold manner in which he had spoken to her when they reached London.

'If I had been wise,' Sorilda thought, 'I would have accepted his offer to live separately, and then I would never have loved him as I do now.'

She knew that to think of him was almost an agony in her breast, to want him and to know that he would never have any idea of it.

She wondered what he was doing. Would he be looking for her, or would he merely think she had run away and the sooner he forgot her the better?

Perhaps he was laughing over it with Peter Lansdown, glad that his marriage had ended so soon and he would no longer be encumbered with a wife.

'He wanted to remain a bachelor,' Sorilda thought, 'and yet one day he might have given me the son he . . . required to carry on the . . . title.'

For the first time, she felt tears come into her eyes at the thought that if he had given her a baby, she would have been close to him. At least for one moment she would have belonged to him and he to her.

The tears in her eyes did not fall, as if she had already died and there was no longer any life in her.

She grew colder and colder.

The rain ceased and there was no longer the sound of it on the iron doors of the crypt, but everything grew damper and she felt as if she were becoming paralysed with it.

"The Duchess has won," she told herself. "I shall die tonight or tomorrow and no-one will ever know!"

She shut her eyes and thought she was falling deeper and deeper into the darkness, and then she could no longer think but only feel that she was already lying in a cold grave. . . .

* * *

As the Earl reached the Hall he said to the footmen:

"One of you run upstairs and tell Mr. Lansdown to come here immediately, and the horses are to come round from the stables at once!"

As the footmen ran to do his bidding, the Earl said as if he had suddenly thought of it:

"Where is Drake?"

"I think he'll be in Her Ladyship's bedroom,

M'Lord," the Butler answered. "He keeps going back there as if to look for Her Ladyship."

"Fetch him!"

Peter Lansdown came down the stairs with Drake at his heels.

"What is it?" he asked as he reached the Earl.

"We are going to the old Abbey," the Earl replied. "It is not far."

He heard the horses at the front door as he spoke, and without another word he went outside and mounted the black stallion.

Without asking any more questions, Peter Lansdown swung himself onto the saddle of the other horse, and with Drake following, the Earl set off.

He rode, not as his friend expected down the drive, but in an unprecedented manner across the lawn until he found the path which led through the shrubberies.

There he was forced to go slowly, bending his head to avoid his hat being knocked off by the over-hanging branches of the trees as he followed the twisting path through the huge banks of rhododendrons which were just coming into bloom.

In a few minutes, however, the Earl emerged onto the rough ground which encircled the ancient Abbey.

Peter Lansdown had seen the ruins before and he wondered why the Earl should think that Sorilda might have come there. Although picturesque, it was a somewhat desolate place even on a sunny day.

Now with the sun sinking and dusk approaching, it looked gloomy and rather sinister and he found himself hoping that Sorilda had not been obliged, because of an accident or some other reason, to stay there the two nights and one day that she had been missing.

The Earl rode into the centre of what at one time had been the main aisle, and there he dismounted.

Peter Lansdown followed his example.

"What are you looking for?" he asked.

"The crypt," the Earl replied. "It is somewhere here."

"You think that Sorilda might have fallen into it by mistake?" Peter Lansdown asked tentatively. "But why? And what was she doing here in the first place?"

The Earl did not answer; he was looking amongst the bushes and then he gave an exclamation.

"Here is the crypt," he said. "But the doors are locked and bolted, so she cannot be here."

He turned away and Peter Lansdown saw the disappointment in his expression.

'He minds! He really minds that he has not found her!' he thought to himself.

He had suspected yesterday and today that the Earl's feelings during the search for Sorilda had not been entirely those of a man who knows it is his duty to find a wife who has disappeared.

'What I have hoped for has happened,' Peter Lansdown thought to himself, though he was afraid that it might be too late now.

"What are you going to do now?" he asked aloud.

"We might as well look round the place while we are here," the Earl said, and his voice was dull.

Then Peter Lansdown gave an exclamation.

"Look at Drake!"

The Earl turned towards the crypt. Drake was scratching violently at the soft earth round the bolted door.

The two men looked at each other. Then as Peter Lansdown reached out to take the reins of the stallion, the Earl bent down and pulled back the bolt which fastened the two iron doors which led to the crypt.

It moved surprisingly easily, as if it had been recently oiled, and then he pulled back first one door and then the other.

Drake gave a little bark of excitement and plunged down the steps into the darkness below, apparently quite unafraid.

The Earl began to follow him. He heard a joyous bark and knew that Drake had found what they sought.

* * *

"Drink a little more, M'Lady, it will do you good," Mrs. Dawson said, but Sorilda shook her head.

The warm soup was delicious and it had seemed to sear away the cold that had enveloped her like a sarcophagus.

She felt as though she had been drinking something warm ever since the Earl had brought her back to the house.

She had only been half-conscious but she had known, as he rode slowly home with his arms round her, that she was where she wanted to be and nothing mattered any more because he had found her.

He had carried her up the stairs and vaguely, though she felt far away and somewhat divorced from reality, she had heard him giving orders for brandy, hot bricks, and a bath.

Then there were maids attending to her, and she had made no effort to do anything but had just let herself drift into the warmth which seemed gradually to be thawing away the cold.

Slowly, very slowly, she felt herself coming back to life.

She had thought she was dead, but with the warmth there was life again in her veins, and first the brandy and then the hot soup began to thaw the ice.

Now she was in bed, her feet were warm and so was the rest of her body, and she felt as if she could not swallow any more.

"No ... thank you ... Mrs. Dawson," she said weakly.

"His Lordship will be disappointed, as he will tell Your Ladyship in a few minutes."

"He is .... coming to ... see me?"

Sorilda could hear the throb in her voice as she asked the question, and Mrs. Dawson replied:

"His Lordship says he'd come up immediately he'd changed and had dinner. Worn out he must be, too, riding all yesterday after being up all night, and starting off at dawn this morning. 'Twas a real fright Your Ladyship gave us."

Sorilda knew that Mrs. Dawson was bursting with curiosity to know what had happened, but at the moment she did not want to talk about it.

She only wanted to know, with an inexpressible joy, that she was alive and that it was the Earl who had saved her.

He had come as she had prayed for him to do and had carried her away to safety before it was too late and she had nearly died from the cold and darkness.

She looked round the bedroom and thought it was the most beautiful place in the whole world.

"Are you quite sure Your Ladyship is warm enough?" Mrs. Dawson asked solicitously.

"It is ... lovely to be so ... warm," Sorilda answered.

She looked towards the fire burning brightly in the hearth and then at the Dresden china candelabra which stood on either side of her dressing-table with half-a-dozen candles burning in each, and she remembered the one little candle which had gone out.

She shut her eyes because it was almost too wonderful to know that she no longer need be afraid. She was home! That was the right word—home! And it was the Earl who had brought her there!

There was a knock at the door and she felt her heart leap.

Mrs. Dawson went to open it.

"Come in, Your Lordship," Sorilda heard her say. "Her Ladyship says she's feeling better."

"That is good," the Earl replied.

He came into the room and Mrs. Dawson went into the passage, closing the door behind her.

For a moment he stood just inside the door, looking at Sorilda lying back against the lace-edged pillows, her red hair falling over her shoulders, her green eyes very large in her pale face.

He walked towards her and impulsively, without even thinking, she put out her hands.

"You... saved me!" she said. "I... prayed for you to... come, but I thought... you would not ... hear me."

The Earl sat down on the side of the bed, holding both her hands in his.

"I think I did hear you," he said, "and I knew that something very wrong and wicked had happened to you. I could feel it almost from the moment it happened."

"I thought I should die and you would... never know where I was," Sorilda said in a low voice.

She felt his fingers tighten on hers.

"That was not meant to happen," he said. "Are you well enough to tell me how you ever got into that damned place?"

"A small... boy took me... there."

The Earl looked puzzled.

"What boy?"

"I do not know. I was on the terrace and he told me I had to go to... Drake at once, and I thought ... he must have had... an... accident."

"Why did you not tell me?"

"You do not... know how many times I have asked myself that... question," Sorilda answered. "But I followed the boy to the crypt, and when he... pointed, I thought... Drake must have... fallen down the steps and... injured himself."

She knew by the expression on the Earl's face that he was angry, and she said:

"It was... very foolish of... me."

"However could you guess that some fiend would lock you in?" he asked.

He saw the expression on Sorilda's face and knew that she was aware who was responsible, who had plotted her destruction.

"Forget it," he said quickly. "We both have to do that, otherwise we shall have no peace, no happiness."

He gave a smile which seemed to transform his face.

"And the only way I can make sure of protecting you is to keep you beside me at all times, both by day and night."

Sorilda looked up at him with a sudden light in her eyes. Then she said a little incoherently:

"You might . . . find that a . . . nuisance."

She thought he was turning something over in his mind before he said:

"You told me that you prayed for me. Did you really want me or just someone to rescue you?"

There was a note in his voice which made Sorilda suddenly feel shy. Her eyes fluttered and she could not look at him.

"I want you to answer that question, Sorilda."

Perhaps it was because she was weak, or perhaps it was impossible to pretend after she had wanted him so agonisingly, but she told the truth.

"I . . . wanted . . . you."

"Did you pray for me?"

"Yes . . . all the . . . time."

"Will you tell me why?"

There was silence and the Earl said:

"Tell me, Sorilda. It is important, and I want to hear the truth."

"I wanted to . . . be . . . with . . . you. I have been so . . . happy since we came to the . . . country."

"I have made you happy?"

Her eyes were very wide as they met his It seemed as if there was no need to put anything into words. He must know what she was feeling, must be aware of her love pouring out towards him.

"I want to tell you something, Sorilda," the Earl said, and his voice was slow and deep.

"What is . . . it?"

"When I lost you I realised how much you had come to mean to me, and I knew it was desperately important for me to find you again so that I could tell you so."

Sorilda's eyes seemed to hold the light of a thousand candles in them.

"Are you . . . saying . . . that . . . you . . . l-like me a . . . little?"

"I am telling you that I love you," the Earl replied, "and in a way I have never loved anyone else."

He gave a sound which was somehow impatient.

"I know you will find it hard to believe that. I know that I have shocked you, that you have despised me, and you had every right to do so. But what I feel for you is something entirely different, and that is not a banal statement that every man makes at some time or other. It is the truth and I want you to believe me."

"I want . . . to! You know I . . . want to, and even if you grow tired of me . . . if you . . . leave me as you have left . . . other . . . women, it will still be . . . like Heaven to . . . have you for . . . even a very . . . little . . . while."

"It is not a question of a very little while," the Earl said gently. "I love you, Sorilda, and actually that is something I have never said to anyone else."

He looked at her as if he thought she would be incredulous, and he added quickly:

"Women have attracted me, I have desired them. There is no need to explain that to you, but I have always known what I gave them was not love, not the real love which I hoped one day I would find, but I thought it would be quite impossible to do so."

"Is that . . . why you never . . . married?"

"Exactly!" the Earl replied. "I swore to myself a long while ago that unless my marriage would be very different from those I saw all round me, I would remain single."

He looked at her searchingly as if he looked deep into her soul, and then he said:

"I want a wife to belong to me completely, forever. I want her to be faithful to me. To be mine exclusively for all time!"

He paused before he said very quietly:

"And I think, Sorilda, I have found her."

Then as she felt that everything that was happening was like some miraculous dream, he bent forward and very gently sought her lips.

It was a tender kiss, a kiss without passion, almost as a man might touch a flower.

To Sorilda it was as if the room were ablaze with a light which came from within themselves and yet was also a part of God.

She felt as if the Earl gave her, with the touch of his lips, everything that she had ever longed for. It was part of the beauty which always moved her and the music that had sung within her heart.

"I love ... you! I love ... you!" she wanted to cry.

Then as she felt herself quiver, the Earl's lips became more possessive, more demanding, and she felt as if he drew her very soul from her body and made it his.

At last, after what seemed an eternity of time, he raised his head.

"I love ... you!" Sorilda cried. "I love ... you! I love ... you!"

"As I love you, my darling."

"It is ... true ... it is really ... true that you ... love ... me?"

"I love you," the Earl replied, "and now you no longer need be afraid I will look after you and protect you, and never will I lose you again."

There was something so moving in his voice that now tears came to her eyes and as she looked at him he seemed enveloped by a haze of glory.

"It is ... so ... wonderful ... so ... perfect," she whispered. "Perhaps after all I am ... dead and am ... in ... Heaven."

As she spoke her voice broke and the tears ran down her cheeks.

The Earl put his arm round her and drew her against him.

"My precious, adorable, beautiful darling. You must not cry. You have been so brave, so incredibly brave, despite all you have been through, and now I want you to be happy and forget it."

He kissed her forehead as he said:

"You are not going to die, you are going to live with me and we are going to find many exciting things to do together."

"Are you . . . sure you want . . . me? I will . . . not . . . bore you?"

"I am quite certain you will never do that," the Earl said. "Peter has kept telling me how intelligent you are, as if I did not realise it myself!"

"I want to be . . . clever for . . . you," Sorilda said simply, "and perhaps . . ."

"What were you going to say?"

"Perhaps I could . . . help you . . . sometimes with all the . . . things you do. It . . . fascinated me when you told me about . . . them."

"I want you to help me," the Earl said. "In fact I want us to do everything together in the future."

It flashed in her mind that in that case there would be no time for him to find further women to attract him.

As if he read her thoughts he laughed and said:

"That is all in the past—forget it, forget everything that has happened until this magical moment. Now there is only one woman who will fill my heart and my life."

"It is too . . . wonderful . . . too . . . perfect."

The Earl took his handkerchief from the breast-pocket of his evening-coat and wiped her cheeks.

"I adore your honest green eyes, your flaming hair, and your white skin. I want to kiss you, my precious darling, all over your perfect body."

He drew in his breath, and as if he made a supreme effort to control his voice, he said more quietly:

"I think, my lovely one, you should go to sleep now. We will talk and make plans tomorrow. One thing we have to decide is where we will spend our honeymoon. I think after all we have been through we are entitled to one!"

"A honeymoon with . . . you would be . . . very . . . marvellous," Sorilda whispered.

Then she turned her face against his shoulder and said in a voice he could barely hear:

"I am only afraid you will . . . find . . . me very . . . ignorant said . . . dull after . . ."

The Earl put his fingers under her chin to turn her face up to his

"You are not to say those words," he said, "nor are you to think such thoughts."

He looked at her searchingly and she saw that his expression was kind and gentle and he looked different from how he had ever looked before.

"Peter said you were the Sleeping Beauty," he said, and his voice was very deep. "I can promise you, my darling, that I am the man who is going to awaken you. It will be the most fascinating and exciting thing I have ever done in my life."

As he spoke, his lips found hers and he kissed her differently from the way he had kissed her before.

Now there was something demanding and what Sorilda knew was passion about his lips, and she felt as if her whole being responded.

A little flame of fire awoke within her, no bigger than the candle-flame, and yet it flickered and burnt its way through her body, up from her breasts and into her throat.

It was a sensation she had never known before, and as the Earl raised his head she whispered:

"Teach . . . me, teach . . . me how to . . . love you so that you will . . . not be . . . disappointed."

"I will teach you about love," the Earl said, and his voice was unsteady "I will awaken my Sleeping Beauty as she will awaken me to a love which is more wonderful than any emotion I have ever before known."

"That is what . . . I . . . want . . . to . . . do!"

"And what you will do, my precious," he answered. "But now you must rest and go to sleep, for you must be very tired."

Sorilda gave a little convulsive murmur, hid her face again, and in a voice he could barely hear she whispered:

"I do . . . not want . . . you to . . . leave . . . me."

She felt him stiffen and become still. Then he said:

"Do you mean that? Do you really mean that, my darling?"

Her voice was barely audible as she murmured:

"When I was in the crypt . . . I pretended . . . that I was in your . . . arms . . . and I felt . . . safe"

"That is what you will always be in the future. But what else did you feel?"

"It was . . . very . . . very . . . exciting, but not as . . . wonderful . . . as really being with . . . you"

His arms held her so tightly that she could barely breathe

"Please . . . stay with . . . me."

The words were barely louder than a sigh but the Earl heard them and there was a sudden fire in his eyes.

"I want you! God knows I want you!" he said. "But I am thinking of you."

His lips twisted with a little smile as he added:

"That is something else I have never done before!"

"I want . . . to . . . be close . . . to you."

As she spoke, Sorilda knew that she could not let him go, could not lose the magic and the wonder of his closeness and his love.

She no longer felt tired; instead, she felt vividly, ecstatically alive.

The Earl had awakened strange sensations within her and his kisses made her feel as if she could fly into the sky with sheer happiness.

He drew her against him as his lips sought hers.

"I love you, my precious little wife, and I want you!" he said. "And neither tonight nor any other night will you ever escape me."

It was as if he made a vow, and Sorilda knew in

that moment that once more she was in prison, but this time it was a prison of the Earl's arms, his hands, his lips, and him—a prison of love.

ABOUT THE AUTHOR

BARBARA CARTLAND, the world's most famous romantic novelist, who is also an historian, playwright, lecturer, political speaker and television personality, has now written over 200 books.

She has also had many historical works published and has written four autobiographies as well as the biographies of her mother and that of her brother Ronald Cartland, who was the first Member of Parliament to be killed in the last war. This book has a preface by Sir Winston Churchill.

Barbara Cartland has sold 100 million books over the world, more than half of these in the U.S.A. She broke the world record in 1975 by writing twenty books, and her own record in 1976 with twenty-one. In addition, her album of love songs has just been published, sung with the Royal Philharmonic Orchestra.

In private life, Barbara Cartland, who is a Dame of the Order of St. John of Jerusalem, has fought for better conditions and salaries for Midwives and Nurses. As President of the Royal College of Midwives (Hertfordshire Branch), she has been invested with the first Badge of Office ever given in Great Britain, which was subscribed to by the Midwives themselves. She has also championed the cause for old people and founded the first Romany Gypsy Camp in the world.

Barbara Cartland is deeply interested in Vitamin Therapy and is President of the British National Association for Health.

BARBARA CARTLAND
PRESENTS
THE ANCIENT WISDOM SERIES

The world's all-time bestselling author of romantic fiction, Barbara Cartland, has established herself as High Priestess of Love in its purest and most traditionally romantic form.

"We have," she says, "in the last few years thrown out the spiritual aspect of love and concentrated only on the crudest and most debased sexual side.

"Love at its highest has inspired mankind since the beginning of time. Civilization's greatest pictures, music, prose and poetry have all been written under the influence of love. This love is what we all seek despite the temptations of the sensuous, the erotic, the violent and the perversions of pornography.

"I believe that for the young and the idealistic, my novels with their pure heroines and high ideals are a guide to happiness. Only by seeking the Divine Spark which exists in every human being, can we create a future built on the foundation of faith."

Barbara Cartland is also well known for her Library of Love, classic tales of romance, written by famous authors like Elinor Glyn and Ethel M. Dell, which have been personally selected and specially adapted for today's readers by Miss Cartland.

"These novels I have selected and edited for my 'Library of Love' are all stories with which the readers can identify themselves and also be assured that right will triumph in the end. These tales elevate and activate the mind rather than debase it as so many modern stories do."

Now, in August, Bantam presents the first four novels in a new Barbara Cartland Ancient Wisdom series. The books are THE FORBIDDEN CITY by Barbara Cartland, herself; THE ROMANCE OF TWO WORLDS by Marie Corelli; THE HOUSE OF FULFILLMENT by L. Adams Beck; and BLACK LIGHT by Talbot Mundy.

"Now I am introducing something which I think is of vital importance at this moment in history. Following my own autobiographical book I SEEK THE MIRACULOUS, which Dutton is publishing in hardcover this summer, I am offering those who seek 'the world behind the world' novels which contain, besides a fascinating story, the teaching of Ancient Wisdom.

"In the snow-covered vastnesses of the Himalayas, there are lamaseries filled with manuscripts which have been kept secret for century upon century. In the depths of the tropical jungles and the arid wastes of the deserts, there are also those who know the esoteric mysteries which few can understand.

"Yet some of their precious and sacred knowledge has been revealed to writers in the past. These books I have collected, edited and offer them to those who want to look beyond this greedy, grasping, materialistic world to find their own souls.

"I believe that Love, human and divine, is the jail-breaker of that prison of selfhood which confines and confuses us . . .

"I believe that for those who have attained enlightenment, super-normal (not super-human) powers are available to those who seek them."

All Barbara Cartland's own novels and her Library of Love are available in Bantam Books, wherever paperbacks are sold. Look for her Ancient Wisdom Series to be available in August.

Barbara Cartland's Library of Love

The World's Great Stories of Romance Specially Abridged by Barbara Cartland For Today's Readers.

- ☐ 11487 **THE SEQUENCE** by Elinor Glyn — $1.50
- ☐ 11468 **THE BROAD HIGHWAY** by Jeffrey Farnol — $1.50
- ☐ 10927 **THE WAY OF AN EAGLE** by Ethel M. Dell — $1.50
- ☐ 10926 **THE REASON WHY** by Elinor Glyn — $1.50
- ☐ 10527 **THE KNAVE OF DIAMONDS** by Ethel M. Dell — $1.50
- ☐ 11465 **GREATHEART** by Ethel M. Dell — $1.50
- ☐ 11895 **HIS OFFICIAL FIANCEE** by Berta Ruck — $1.50
- ☐ 11369 **THE BARS OF IRON** by Ethel M. Dell — $1.50
- ☐ 11370 **MAN AND MAID** by Elinor Glyn — $1.50
- ☐ 11391 **THE SONS OF THE SHEIK** by E. M. Hull — $1.50
- ☐ 12140 **THE LION TAMER** by E. M. Hull — $1.50
- ☐ 11467 **THE GREAT MOMENT** by Elinor Glyn — $1.50
- ☐ 12436 **LEAVE IT TO LOVE** by Pamela Wynne — $1.50
- ☐ 11816 **THE PRICE OF THINGS** by Elinor Glyn — $1.50
- ☐ 11821 **TETHERSTONES** by Ethel M. Dell — $1.50

Buy them at your local bookstore or use this handy coupon for ordering:

Barbara Cartland

The world's bestselling author of romantic fiction. Her stories are always captivating tales of intrigue, adventure and love.

☐ 02972	A DREAM FROM THE NIGHT	$1.25
☐ 02987	CONQUERED BY LOVE	$1.25
☐ 10971	THE RHAPSODY OF LOVE	$1.50
☐ 10715	THE MARQUIS WHO HATED WOMEN	$1.50
☐ 10975	A DUEL WITH DESTINY	$1.50
☐ 10976	CURSE OF THE CLAN	$1.50
☐ 10977	PUNISHMENT OF A VIXEN	$1.50
☐ 11101	THE OUTRAGEOUS LADY	$1.50
☐ 11168	A TOUCH OF LOVE	$1.50
☐ 11169	THE DRAGON AND THE PEARL	$1.50
☐ 11962	A RUNAWAY STAR	$1.50
☐ 11690	PASSION AND THE FLOWER	$1.50
☐ 12292	THE RACE FOR LOVE	$1.50
☐ 12566	THE CHIEFTAIN WITHOUT A HEART	$1.50

Buy them at your local bookstore or use this handy coupon for ordering:

Barbara Cartland

The world's bestselling author of romantic fiction. Her stories are always captivating tales of intrigue, adventure and love.